BOOK 2
DIMWORLD
SERIES

WHEN GOOD PLANS GO BAD

Books by J. Boyd Long

Genesis Dimension, book 1 of the *DimWorld* Series

When Good Plans Go Bad, book 2 of the *DimWorld* Series

WHEN GOOD PLANS GO BAD

J. BOYD LONG

MAD GOAT PRESS

MAD GOAT
PRESS

For Erica, who is also not from this planet.
Or, at least, not from this dimension.

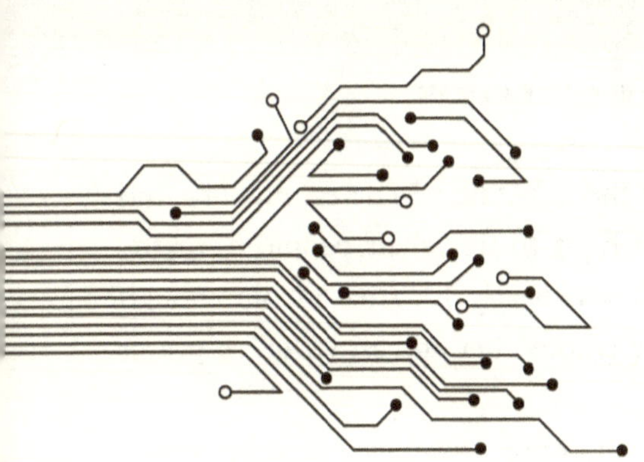

PROLOGUE

5 years earlier

Piercing screams filled the air, adding to the mounting panic that churned in Mazik's stomach. Smoke from the burning warehouse billowed into the courtyard, burning his eyes and throat as he ran. People scattered in every direction, creating chaos in the work camp. He tripped over a body and crashed into the packed dirt. Bits of gravel gouged his skin, but he ignored the pain that flared up his arm and sprang back to his feet. The body he had fallen over wore a DimCorp guard's uniform, so he dismissed it and ran on, desperately searching for his father.

The slave rebellion was in full motion now. Bribri slaves fought with the DimCorp guards, trying to overwhelm them with numbers to make up for the lack of proper weapons. Mazik clapped his hands to his ears as a sudden barrage of gunfire erupted in front of him. The sound was deafening, much louder than anything he had ever heard. His knees buckled as terror consumed him.

"Mazik!"

He heard his mother's scream over the ringing in his ears and twisted his head around. The women were herding the children down an alley towards the front gate. He knew he was supposed to be with them, but he was determined to find his father and help him fight to free their people from the DimCorp plantation. He was nearly 13, after all, old enough to make a difference. He ignored her and said a quick prayer for courage.

The guard who was shooting must have heard her shout. Mazik watched, helpless, as the guard swung his rifle around towards the fleeing women and children. Sound became muffled, as if everything were suddenly far away, as the barrel spit fire once, twice, three times.

A moment later, Mazik's father appeared. He sprang on the guard from behind, driving him to the ground. Mazik lay frozen in place, his heart pounding so hard he thought his chest might burst. The men rolled on the ground, punching and clawing at each other. Mazik felt a ray of hope as his father managed to get the guard in a choke hold, and his paralysis broke. He jumped to his feet to help his father, but before he could take a step, the guard pulled a knife from his boot and began stabbing his father repeatedly, slashing his arms and legs.

Mazik charged as his father fell back, blood pouring to the dusty ground beneath him. The guard knelt and plunged the knife into his father's chest just as Mazik sprang onto his back, trying to replicate the chokehold his father had used. The guard pulled the knife out of his father's chest with one hand, grasping Mazik's arm with the other. With a lightning-quick move, he rolled to one side, pulling Mazik over his shoulder at the same time. Mazik crashed to the ground beside his father as the knife came rushing towards his face. He whipped his head to the side. Searing pain burned his face as the knife sliced through his cheek. The coppery taste of blood flooded his mouth, threatening to choke him.

"Bader!"

The voice of Vincent Macalister roaring across the courtyard stopped Mazik's heart in his chest. The guard hesitated, wiped the knife on Mazik's shirt, and climbed to his feet.

"Right here, boss," he shouted.

"Get over here and guard the warehouse. Don't let anybody get to the Gate, you hear me?"

"Yes, boss."

Bader gave Mazik a savage kick in the ribs and jogged across the courtyard. Mazik gagged, spitting blood out as he gasped for air.

"Where the hell is my fire team?"

Macalister's shouting echoed in Mazik's ears as the world turned gray around him. Soon, the only things he was aware of were agonizing pain in his side, his burning cheek, and his father's body beside him, and he realized he was about to pass out. If that happened, he would be dead. He forced himself to his feet, holding a hand to his slashed cheek, and limped towards the alley after his mother and the others.

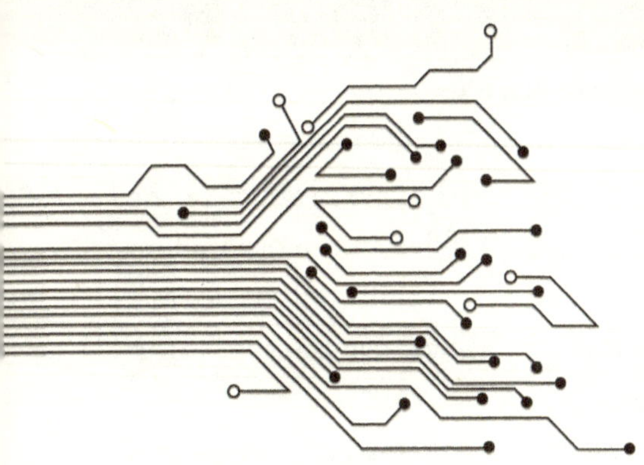

CHAPTER 1

Quentin sprinted across the dooryard in front of the cabin, trying to look everywhere at once as he fled into the jungle. It was impossible to be cautious once he was in the trees. There were just too many places that someone could be hiding. The palm fronds created a natural wall around him, hiding any unknown danger behind a dark green screen. When he got to the pre-arranged meeting place, it was empty. *Where the hell is Eissa?*

There was no time to wait. If she wasn't there, he had no choice but to go on. Tree limbs grabbed at him as he bolted down the trail. He burst into the clearing in front of the DimGate and attempted to do a somersault as he dove around the left side of the door. It was an awkward, graceless roll, but he somehow managed to wind up on his feet.

There was no one hiding behind the door as he had expected there to be, and it took him a moment to shift mental gears. He'd been ready to fight, coaching himself through his first three moves as he ran, but now he had to skip all that and advance to the next goal: escape from this dimension. *Adapt and overcome, Q. You can do this.*

He opened the control panel for the DimGate and powered it up, cursing the slow nature of the computer. *Come on, come on.* There was still no sign of Eissa. He dreaded the thought of leaving her behind, but he had no idea where she was, and no time to look for her. He filled in the destination dimension fields on the touchscreen and activated the door. A quick glance back up the trail confirmed that Eissa wasn't in sight, and his heart sank.

He opened the DimGate a few inches and peered through the crack. There weren't any buses or trains about to smash through the door, so he pushed it open, crossed into Dimension 443, and slammed it shut. On this side of the DimGate, the wind was whipping on the roof of the Diablo Tower, and he barely heard Eissa's taunting voice as he opened the control panel to disable the door.

"What took you so long? I've been here for ten minutes."

He spun around, unsure if he had imagined it or not, but there she was, standing with Bob and Tocho on the other side of the roof. He stared in disbelief.

"What the hell are you doing on this side of the Gate? We were supposed to meet in the jungle. And how could you have gotten here faster than me? That's not even possible." He went back over his steps, trying to figure out where he might have lost some time. He had gotten his hands untied quickly, and while it took him a minute to get the first floorboard up, the rest came up easy, and he had crawled out from under the cabin within five minutes of the starting whistle.

The smirk on Eissa's face told him she was feeling smug about beating him in yet another training exercise. She sauntered over as he disabled the DimGate, Bob and Tocho trailing behind her with sheepish grins of their own.

"Not only is it possible, my dear Quentin, it's also five wins in a row for yours truly. Count them, five big ones." She held up a hand, her fingers spread wide. "I believe that means you'll be doing my chores for the next three days, minion."

The wall of flying cars on either side of the building made it difficult to focus on his humiliating loss, even though he'd seen the spectacle repeatedly over the last week. Las Vegas wasn't the kind of place you could tune out, especially in this dimension. Massive video screens covered the skyscrapers around them, advertising the treasures and adventures to be had in the casinos below, and displaying giant naked women with impossibly long legs dancing in shows every hour of the day and night. He shook his head with a grin, looking back at her.

"Well, I don't know how you did it, but you got me." He leaned in as they gathered in a circle beside the DimGate. They had the roof of the Diablo Tower to themselves, as usual. It wasn't a great place to hang out, as the noise from the wind and the traffic made conversation difficult. "Why don't we go down to the Cosmos Kitchen and try out this amazing food we've heard so much about, and you can tell me how you're cheating."

They made their way over to the airlift at the edge of the roof. Quentin brushed the dirt off his shoulder from his attempted combat roll and ran his hands over his hair. His normally-short buzzcut was beginning to grow out, and he was going to have to find a place to get a haircut soon. Now that the DimGate was working reliably, that would be much easier to accomplish.

The doors hissed open, and they stepped onto the airlift. They had been crossing into this dimension all week in their training missions, but this was the first time they had left the roof of the Diablo Tower. The lift climbed the side of the tower from ground level to roof, and its walls were clear, allowing them a spectacular view of the city. The doors closed behind them, sealing off the turbulence of the roof.

"You'll want to hold on to the rail," Tocho said, pushing the button for the ground level. "It goes down pretty fast."

Quentin grinned as Eissa grabbed the rail with both hands. His own hands were in his pockets, and his thoughts were still on her dislike for amusement park rides when the floor fell out from beneath him. His stomach shot into his throat as his feet left the floor, and he floated, not quite hitting the ceiling, but not touching the floor. There was an initial moment of panic, but it quickly became fun. The city beyond was a blur of color and shapes, and the only thing he could really see was the backs of the other three as they grasped the handrail and looked out over Vegas. He started to get Eissa's attention, but then decided to see if he could get into a funny pose first.

Just as he got his hands out of his pockets, the airlift began to slow, and his feet gently came back down to the floor. He grabbed the rail to steady himself, relieved that he hadn't had time to turn upside down, or something equally ridiculous. He would have come crashing down as the lift slowed, and probably hurt himself. *Don't let your inner child come out to play on the airlift, Q.* He laughed at himself as the doors opened.

Eissa pried her hands off the rail and turned around. Her face was pale, and she clearly hadn't enjoyed the airlift ride. Quentin put his arm around her shoulders and gave her a squeeze.

"Come on, champ. A five-time winner like you can't puke on the way to dinner, it's unbecoming of your station. Think about all the kids out there looking up to you."

Eissa elbowed him lightly in the ribs. "Yeah, yeah, kiss my ass." She followed Bob and Tocho out onto the street.

Las Vegas was even more overwhelming on the ground level. The street was wide, much wider than any city street in Quentin's dimension. Lines of automated cars maneuvered around one another and the thousands of pedestrians. On the other side of the street was a station for the train that he had seen from the roof. It ran in a clear tube above the street level. Quentin stared in amazement as a train left the station and shot out of sight within seconds.

"That's the Mag-Vac," Bob said. "Pretty impressive, huh?"

Quentin nodded mutely. It put the mono-rails from his dimension to shame.

"It's a vacuum tube," Bob explained. "Almost no air in it, so no wind resistance. The cross-country Mag-Vacs run something like 1,800 miles an hour. You can go from here to New York in about two hours, London in three, and Beijing is about four hours."

"Holy shit." Quentin tried to imagine what he would do with that kind of technology available. In theory, you could get off work on Friday, spend the weekend anywhere in the world, and be back to work on Monday morning. How cool would that be? "That's almost as good as having a teleporter."

"Oh no," Eissa said. "You can't beat a teleporter. Instant transportation."

"I'm not saying it's equal, but it's still pretty damn good."

Eissa winked at him. "I'll give you that. It's still pretty good."

Tocho steered them to a door at the base of the tower. A doorman in a dark green tuxedo and a top hat greeted them and ushered them into a foyer. There were massive chandeliers hanging from the ceiling, and deep carpeting absorbed the sound of muted conversations. Another man in a tuxedo came out from a side room and intercepted them.

"Good evening, gentlemen and lady."

Bob bowed low, somehow managing to not look completely ridiculous. "Good evening, sir. Four for dinner, if you please."

"Of course. If you would please accompany me, we will arrange suitable dining attire." He swept them into the side room with a flourish.

The room was filled with racks of suits and evening gowns. Quentin looked down at his dirty plaid shirt and stained khakis and felt shamefully out of place. He caught Eissa looking at her dirty clothes, and they shared an embarrassed grin.

"Don't worry," Tocho said. "This is what they do. That's why they have all these clothes. They don't expect you to show up in a tux."

Two small men appeared out of the back and began taking quick measurements on them. After a moment, one of them turned to Eissa.

"If the lady would accompany me to the gowns, and select a style?" he said, holding his arm out.

"No chance, Jack. You can set me up in a tuxedo, too. Preferably something purple."

Quentin cringed, but the little man handled her like a true professional. With a knowing wink, he placed his hand on the small of her back and guided her toward a rack of tuxedos against the wall.

"We have an excellent selection in purple. Are you a periwinkle, or a plum?"

Eissa looked a bit flustered. "I'm a periwinkle, for sure. Nothing too dark."

Tocho roared with laughter. "She thought she was going to surprise him with that? You have to try a lot harder than that in this dimension." His eyes danced with mirth. "Hell, I might go for purple, too." He followed them, still laughing.

Quentin glanced at Bob with a grin. Maybe it was an endorphin rush from essentially falling from the roof to the ground in the airlift, or maybe it was that they were in a bustling city around other people after being alone on the island for a month, but he was enormously enjoying himself. Bob smiled back at him, clearly enjoying himself, too.

Once they all had suits picked out, they were taken to shower and primp. This was an unexpected bonus for Quentin, and he turned the water temperature up as high as he could stand it. While the island life had a lot of things going for it, their outdoor shower had very low water pressure, and the water was heated by the sun. It worked, but it was a poor substitute for the luxury of a really good shower. By the time he got out, he felt like a new man. He joined the others back in the clothing room.

Eissa was standing in front of a full-length mirror. She was wearing an exceptionally well-cut periwinkle tuxedo, and it fit her like it had been tailored for her. Her long black hair was pulled back in an intricate braid, and the tailor was pinning a small pale flower to her lapel. It felt strange to Quentin to think of her this way, but she looked stunning.

"Damn, Eissa, you look incredible. I don't think I've ever seen you dressed up like this before."

She beamed at him. "Thanks, Q. You look pretty snappy, yourself."

Tocho wandered up beside her. He was wearing a black tuxedo with royal purple satin lapels and a matching satin vest and bow tie. He looked quite dashing with his hair in a braid. The tailor turned to him.

"Would the gentleman care for a handkerchief in his jacket pocket?"

Tocho's face lit up with a huge smile. "Yes, yes I would."

"And what color would the gentleman prefer?"

Tocho thought for a moment. "Orange."

"Left pocket, or right?"

"Right."

The tailor nodded and fussed with it until it was just right.

Quentin turned to Bob and leaned in close. "How are we going to pay for all this?"

Bob's eyes sparkled in amusement. He pointed to a bench near the door, and they walked over and sat down. "Funding isn't a problem for us. One of the things Rupert got us, besides our own DimGate, was a bank account full of DimCorp money."

Quentin looked at Bob quickly, then looked away. They were rich? How did that work? Did money move between dimensions? He had started with one question, and now he had a hundred. Bob chuckled softly.

"I can hear the gears grinding in your head, Quentin. It's just normal electronic banking. Since DimCorp owns the bank, we can use our card in any dimension where there's a branch. It's no different than what you're used to, you just have to know which banks are DimCorp banks."

Quentin nodded. Having money available changed his whole perception of their situation. In some ways he appreciated the irony of DimCorp unknowingly funding them, but it also grated on him how much easier everything became when you didn't have to worry about how you were going to pay for things. Having spent his entire life on the other side of the coin, living from one paycheck to the next, he wasn't sure how to feel about it. It would be ridiculous to not use DimCorp's money just on principle, right? Yes, that would be ridiculous.

The maître d' appeared at the door with a flourish. "Good evening, lady and gentlemen. If the party is ready to be seated?" His heavy French accent perfectly complimented his role, and he swept his arm towards the door, his white-gloved hand outstretched.

They followed him into the dining room, weaving between tables and waiters laden with trays of food. The room was huge, but it was divided into pockets of ambience with low walls and small trees in a way that made it seem cozy and private. They arrived at their table and were seated as the maître d' made a show of fussing with the tablecloth and accoutrements. He smiled at Tocho as he leaned past him to light a candle. "I love your suit, it's very fetching."

Tocho beamed. "Why, thank you, you're very kind."

Quentin blushed, and quickly looked down at the menu. Watching Tocho flirt with a guy that was at least forty years younger than him was a little awkward. His stomach growled in anticipation of a good meal, something other than fish, for a change. Granted, the diet on the island had done him good. He had lost some weight, and the training regime included more exercise than he had ever done in his life. Still, it would be nice to eat some chicken or pork.

Once the maître d' had announced the specials and left them to look over the menu, Quentin took a moment to look around. Outside, this dimension was loaded with futuristic technology. In here though, in what was probably one of the finest restaurants there was, it looked like it could be in any dimension. There were no robots delivering food, no screens on the table to order from, nothing advanced at all.

Quentin cleared his throat and glanced around to make sure there was no one within earshot. "I sort of expected something different. This is really nice, but it's not what I thought it would be like at all."

Bob raised his eyebrows. "What were you expecting?"

Quentin shrugged. "You know, some kind of advanced technology. Floating trays, automated servers, something like that."

"Oh, no," Bob said. "I think you're misunderstanding the situation. Every fast food place in town is automated. Delivery is automated. Cars are automated. Shopping is automated. That's commonplace. The very best that money can buy is personal service from another human being. That's what they offer here, the personal touch. It's a rare commodity." He took a roll and passed the bread basket to Quentin.

That was a lot to think about. In Quentin's dimension, automated services like self-checkout and automated ordering kiosks at restaurants were still new technology, and sort of a novelty. The idea that it might become so common that a real live waiter was the novelty made him take a mental step back.

"They give you a wicked-awesome tux to wear, too," Eissa pointed out. "That has some value."

"To be sure," Bob said with a grin. "Especially when you've been on the island for a month."

The menu was also surprising to Quentin. He was expecting exotic things that he'd never heard of, and while there were a few items like that, most of it looked familiar. There was a page dedicated to steaks, a page for seafood, salads, and all the other usual fare. He wasn't normally a steak eater, but this was a special circumstance, and it sounded appealing. He glanced at the dessert page, and then flipped back to the steaks.

"They're really specific about their steaks," he said. The information beside each steak option was different than what he was used to. "They list all these different fat compounds and stuff. Weird."

Tocho leaned forward conspiratorially. "That's how you choose the flavor," he explained. "This meat is grown in a lab, it's not actually from live animals."

Quentin glanced at Eissa, then back to Tocho. "Are you serious?"

Tocho nodded.

"Oh my God, that's awesome," Eissa said. "Somebody finally did it."

Quentin grinned, nodding his head. This dimension was winning him over pretty quickly. Clean energy, clean food, high-speed transportation that didn't require fossil fuels, there was a lot to like. "I might need some help with the flavor selection, then. Any recommendations?"

"Mmm," Bob mumbled around a mouthful of bread. "P3 is a pork-based fat. You can't go wrong with that, especially on a filet mignon. I guarantee it will be the best steak you ever had."

Quentin glanced over the selection of side items and finalized his order just as the waiter came and delivered drinks. When he had taken their dinner orders and walked away, Quentin changed discussion topics. "Alright Eissa, tell me how you got through the DimGate so fast."

Eissa set her glass down and dabbed at her smiling mouth with a napkin. "It was stupid easy, really. When Tocho took you into the cabin, Bob was supposed to take me down to the beach and tie me up, right?"

Quentin nodded.

"Well, I decided not to go to the beach. We're training for escape skills, so I escaped. I used that ninja hip toss we learned on Bob right there in front of the cabin, and just walked to the DimGate and crossed over. Two minutes, job done."

Bob grunted. "Took me by surprise, I'll admit. Tocho had to help me up. By then, the plan was out the window, so we just came on over to wait for you. I wasn't about to wrestle with you after Eissa knocked me on my ass."

They laughed. Quentin knew he shouldn't be surprised, but he couldn't help feeling a little peeved. That was just Eissa being Eissa, but still, it sucked being the only person in the game who followed the protocol. "Well, since you didn't play by the rules, I shouldn't have to do your chores."

"You go ahead and follow the rules, Quentin. I'm going to survive." She scrunched up her nose and stuck her tongue out at him. "In case you've forgotten, one of us got captured by DimCorp, and one of us performed a daring rescue, and it wasn't me that got captured, so don't criticize my technique."

Quentin sighed. She reminded him about that at least three times a week. He'd given up arguing with her about it or defending himself. It was better to let her get it out of her system, so they could move on. He had to smile as he picked up his glass. Eissa might not color inside the lines the way he did, but it was hard to argue with her results. She had saved his butt in the Genesis Dimension, which was the worst jam he'd ever been in, but she'd gotten him out of a lot of other scrapes and tight spots over the years, too. When they were kids, they'd gone exploring in an old, abandoned cement plant. Quentin fell through a hole in the floor, and she made a rope out of their jean jackets and pulled him up. It took years for her to stop reminding him about that one.

His mood brightened at the memory, and he pushed the irritation away. This was a special dinner, signifying the end of their training and the beginning of their next mission. It certainly wasn't the time or the place to get an attitude.

Tocho tapped his glass with his fork, breaking the spell of the moment. "I'd like to propose a toast. We've come a long way in a short time, and I'm proud of us all for what we're doing. So, here's to the Fearsome Four." He raised his glass in a salute.

"Here, here," Bob said, raising his glass. Quentin and Eissa followed his lead. "To the Fearsome Four."

Quentin raised his glass next, and the others looked at him expectantly. "I just wanted to thank everyone. I've had to change the way I think about a lot of things, and you've all taught me a lot. I'm looking forward to our mission tomorrow, and I'm proud and honored to be a part of this team."

The others intonated affirmations, clinking glasses. "And to Eissa," he added. "Who always has my back." He winked at her and raised his glass.

The food arrived, and any further toasts were abandoned in favor of eating. Bob was right. It was the best steak Quentin ever had.

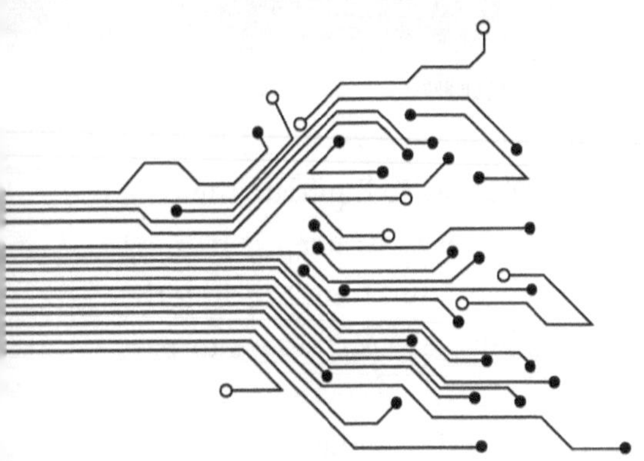

CHAPTER 2

Vincent Macalister sat behind his desk, brooding. The barren walls of his office seemed to reflect his sullen mood. He had known this was going to happen from the moment the DimGate powered back up two weeks ago. At some point the DimCorp brass would send someone through the Gate to see what he had done with their cacao plantation for the last three years.

In all reality, the meeting had gone well. After all, it wasn't as if he had shut down the plantation and gone fishing. No, quite the opposite. He smiled to himself, thinking about how impressed the corporate messenger had been. The cacao grove was almost twice the size that it had been when the Gate shut down, and now there were sugarcane fields, too. They were producing chocolate like a goddamn factory out here in the middle of the jungle, and trading on a major scale with the Inka and the Aztec both.

Of course, he hadn't *fully* explained everything he had done. Some secrets were better kept as secrets, like the gold. He hadn't mentioned the gold. That was the real problem here. Three years of being cut off from DimCorp had been a boon, and he was making a fortune trading chocolate for gold. Now that the DimGate was working again, his whole operation was going to have to change, and he wasn't sure he was ready to retire yet. He had to figure out a way to liquidate the gold he had, and hopefully, figure out a way to keep it coming in without DimCorp taking it away from him. Sending the cacao to headquarters was fine, but he wasn't about to part with the gold.

There was a knock at the door. He grabbed a pen and pulled some paperwork over to the middle of the desk.

"What is it?"

Morgan Gage opened the door slightly and poked his head in. "You wanted to see me, boss?" His dark hair was combed neatly, and his uniform and boots were immaculate, as always.

Macalister glanced up from the paperwork. "Sit down," he grunted, nodding at the folding chair across the desk.

Gage closed the door and sat down. Macalister pretended to be busy reading the pages in front of him, jotting a note here and there. Gage didn't fidget as he waited, nor did Macalister expect him to. This was a battle of wills, and while Gage was experienced, he never got to win this game. This was one of the tools Macalister used to remind Gage of his place in the grand scheme of things. The longer Gage had to wait on Macalister, the more time he had to think about who was in charge.

Morgan Gage was his second in command. He was a good leader, at least in the respect that the men responded well to him, but he was weak, spineless. He had come from the Academy four years ago with a lot of big ideas, such as trying to be friends with the guards and the slaves both, which made him look soft. He didn't think it was important to discipline the slaves publicly. Things like that.

Macalister knew that Gage thought he could do a better job of running the operation. Gage had even begun to question

Macalister about various things lately, and that was totally unacceptable. He had complete control over Gage while the DimGate had been out of operation, but now that it was back up, he was going to have to change direction slightly. It galled him to approach Gage in any way other than with the iron fist, which was his primary method of diplomacy, but this was a special situation, and a room full of gold hung in the balance. He let the silence drag out for another minute.

"The corporate monkey said they'll be ready to start pulling cacao out of here in about a month," he said at last, tossing the pen on the desk with a sigh and putting the papers in a drawer.

"He seemed pretty satisfied with things on his tour," Gage said, glancing up at him. "The part that I saw, at least."

Macalister shrugged. "He fucking-well ought to be."

"So, what are we going to do about everything?" Gage's expression was unreadable.

Silence fell over the room as Macalister looked out the window. This was a delicate tightrope he had to walk. He needed Gage to commit to him. Gage knew everything that was going on, and had the ability to sink him if he blabbed to Corporate about the gold. It might be best to just kill him, but that wouldn't sit well with the rest of the guards. Better to beat him into submission or find a way to incriminate him, so he couldn't blow the whistle without taking himself down, too.

"Well, that's what we gotta figure out. They don't want the chocolate, at least not right now; they just want the cacao nibs. The Inka and the Aztec want the chocolate, though, and they'll give us all the goddamn gold in the world to get it. The way I see it, we ought to figure out a way to do both."

Gage's eyes widened, and Macalister grinned inwardly.

"That's going to be tough," Gage said. "Corporate is going to want all the cacao we can produce, right? We don't really have any way to do both."

"We'll have to make some adjustments. I think we'll have to turn two of the cane fields into cacao groves. We'll cut down on the chocolate production and raise the price, so we won't lose too much on that side, and DimCorp will just have to be patient while the two new groves get going. Hell, they'll still be getting just about as much as they were before."

Gage shifted uneasily in the chair. "You mean that we keep some of the cacao, and keep making chocolate on the sly?"

"That's called a fringe perk," Macalister said carefully. It was time to dangle the bait. "It's an unwritten rule, but that's how they expect us to supplement what they give us to live on. Everyone does it; you just can't be obvious about it. Hell, you want some of that gold for your retirement, right? So, how do we make that happen?"

He watched as Gage digested the idea. The anger that he always felt towards Gage rumbled just below the surface, and he forced it back down. He needed to get through this without losing his temper, regardless of how maddening Gage was.

"We've got one cane field empty that we just cut last week, and another one that's due in a few weeks," Gage said. "I can pull some workers from the mill and have them take cuttings and start planting cacao in Field 6."

Macalister nodded.

"I still think DimCorp's going to question the low amount we're sending them," Gage said. "The guy today saw how many fields we have."

Macalister's temper flared. "DimCorp will take what we give them. If we tell them there's ten bushels a week, then that's what they get." He stopped, reminding himself to stay in control.

"What if they send an auditor over?"

"The auditors don't know shit about cacao. All they'll see is piles of beans fermenting in one spot, and sheets of them drying in another spot. They don't know how much is there." Macalister got up and walked over to the window and looked out over the square. "No, the problem is going to be when they want to count the warehouse, and there's a pirate ship's worth of gold treasure sitting in a locked room in the corner. That's the part we gotta figure out."

"I take it you didn't tell him about the gold, then."

"Fuck no, I didn't tell him about the gold." Macalister spun around, his face livid. "I've been slaving away in this miserable goddamn jungle for fifteen years. They didn't do any of the work that earned that gold. They didn't plan, they didn't struggle, they didn't try to teach a bunch of goddamn cavemen how to make chocolate. They didn't go meet with the chief of the spear-chucking locals and try to negotiate a trade deal without getting sacrificed by their goddamn priests. You think I'm giving them my gold? You're out of your fucking mind."

Gage remained silent, his face impassive. Macalister dropped back into his chair and ran his fingers through his hair. He blew out a deep breath and tried to get his temper under control. The sweat trickling down his back didn't help his mood. Black spots danced in front of his eyes, and he rubbed his face, determined to get through the conversation.

"Now that the Gate's up, we're going to start getting supplies again in a month or two. I'm changing the price of the chocolate. It's all gold from here on out."

Gage stiffened in his chair, and Macalister glared at him. "Look, Gage. We had a windfall with this chocolate business. Now, we can be good boys and shut it down, and hope that what we've got is enough to retire on, or we can keep going. Now, personally, I'd rather live in the Caribbean somewhere when I'm old, sitting on the beach with young girls running around. How about you? Do you want to freeze your ass off in Ohio, or do you want to retire in style?"

"The beach sounds nice," Gage mumbled, looking at the floor.

Macalister blew out a breath. If he really intended to share the gold with Gage, this conversation would be unbearable. There was a small amount of joy to be had in knowing that he was keeping it all for himself, and he held on to that joy tightly.

"Send a runner to the Inka. Tell him the price is going up, and we only want gold this time, no clothes, no food."

"We need that food, boss. The supplies aren't here yet. Besides, some of the food we get from the Inka is a lot better than what Corporate used to send us."

"Send the fucking runner!" Macalister screamed. His face contorted with rage, and a fleck of spittle flew from his lips. "I'm the motherfucker in charge here, do you understand that? Don't you ever question me again, Gage. Goddammit, you make me so mad I can't think straight."

"Sorry, boss."

Gage stood and walked to the door. Macalister stared out the window and ignored him until he closed the door. He felt a headache growing behind his left eye.

The corporate monkey had assured him that he had a paycheck coming with the three years of backpay on it. He needed to figure out how to cross over to the Genesis Dimension, empty his bank account and get back here without raising any red flags. Then he had to find a way to get all the gold melted down into bars that he could transport by himself. After that, he needed to find a dimension he could escape to for his retirement. The headache was getting worse.

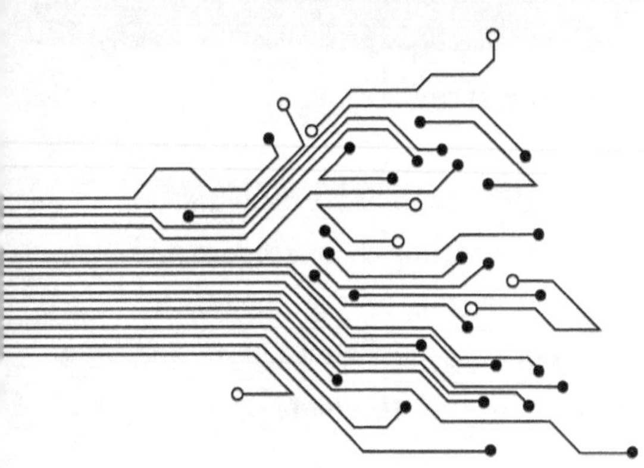

CHAPTER 3

Quentin woke up early, as he usually did. The island seemed incredibly still and quiet after spending the previous evening in Vegas, and he lay in bed for a few minutes just listening to it. Dimension 443 was as different from this one as it could be, and while there was certainly some excitement in the lights and the hustle and bustle, there was something to be said for the serenity that came with a deserted island, too. For instance, he probably wouldn't be able to sleep beside an open window in Las Vegas, no matter how nice the temperature was.

Soon the urge for coffee overrode the desire to stay in bed, and he crept over into the kitchen area, trying not to wake the others as he added wood to the stove and coaxed the few remaining coals back to life. Before they had come back to the island last night, they had done some shopping, and he was excited to try out some new coffee beans. It only took a few minutes for the kettle to heat up, and soon he was seated on the porch with a steaming mug.

Their plan for today was to revisit a dimension that Bob and Tocho had gone to about five years before. Back then, DimCorp had been running a cacao plantation out in the jungle, using a small tribe of indigenous people called the Bribri as slave labor. Bob and Tocho helped the Bribri overthrow the guards and escape. It seemed like a good place to get some hands-on training with a group of people who had gone through the whole process of asserting their freedom and independence from DimCorp and starting over on their own.

Quentin jumped as the door closed behind him, and turned to see Bob limping over to his rocking chair.

"Good morning."

Bob nodded, blowing on his coffee as he carefully sat down.

"Is your knee bothering you again?" Quentin asked.

"Just a little stiff," Bob said. "Eissa really put one on me yesterday, when she did that hip toss." He held up his mug to Quentin. "Good choice on the coffee, that's very nice."

Quentin returned the salute and took another swallow. It was a strong, dark coffee, and it smelled just as good as it tasted. "Yep, I really like it."

They sat in silence, enjoying the coffee. The sun was just beginning to turn the horizon pink behind the palm trees. This had become their routine over the last month, sharing coffee and the sunrise before they got started on the day's activities. They didn't talk much, as nothing needed to be said.

After breakfast, they finished packing their backpacks with supplies. They had no idea what the situation was in the Bribri's dimension, so they were taking everything they might need to stay for a few days. Eissa had almost all their medical supplies packed, and they had enough food to last them for a week. The sun was well up in the sky when they assembled in front of the DimGate.

"Tocho," Bob called out. "Are you coming?"

They glanced back up the trail towards the cabin. The mid-morning sun was still blocked by the thick forest canopy, casting deep shadows through the woods. A moment later, Tocho came into view.

"Sorry, I had to pee again. Getting old is hell. Where are we?"

"I'm about to run through the startup on the DimGate, and you're about to give the safety briefing." Bob stepped around the side of the DimGate and opened the panel.

"Ok, let's see." Tocho glanced at Quentin, then Eissa. "We all have our backpacks, yes? Eissa, you've got your medical stuff?"

"Yep, I'm loaded down with pretty much everything we have."

"I had to put some of the bandaging in my pack," Quentin said. "But yeah, I think we've got everything we could need to simulate a rescue mission, or whatever."

Tocho nodded. "Now then. We haven't been to this dimension in five years. The last time we were there was the day they revolted, and we were only there for the beginning of that, so we don't have any idea what's going on with them these days. Hopefully Viho is still the chief, but we'll proceed cautiously, just to be on the safe side."

Bob poked his head around the side of the DimGate. "Hopefully they haven't moved. It's possible they might not even be there anymore, or that they got absorbed into the Cabecar tribe, or maybe even by the Aztecs."

"The Aztecs?" Quentin's eyebrows shot up.

Bob flashed a grin. "You bet. This is another dimension where the Spanish were unsuccessful in the Americas. The Aztec empire is still going strong. The Inka empire is too, down south. I've been looking forward to going back and doing a bit of exploring for a long time."

Quentin sighed. There was so much about history that he hadn't retained, or hadn't even learned, back when he was in school. While stuff like the Aztec empire had been interesting, it hadn't been something that he thought he would need to know someday. Not for the first time, he wished he could access the internet and do some quick research before they continued.

"Anyway," Tocho continued. "We're going to be careful. Once we find the Bribri, we'll see what the situation is and go from there. Hopefully they'll be up for some training exercises, but we'll walk on eggshells until we're sure."

Bob activated the DimGate. It hummed deeply for a moment, and a loud click indicated that it was ready. "We should be in the woods just up from the lake. Go ahead and check it out, Tocho."

Quentin and Eissa stepped to the side as Tocho cracked the door open. He peered through the gap, and a moment later he slipped through to the other side. Quentin stepped up to the open door, watching carefully for any sign of danger.

The forest on the other side of the door was in stark contrast to the jungle on the island side. Instead of the palmetto plants that he had become accustomed to on the island, ferns dominated on the other side. Everything was green and wet. Tocho reappeared, waving them forward through the DimGate.

Quentin turned back to Bob and Eissa. "All set, let's go."

They crossed over to Dimension 214 and stood in a loose circle as Bob disabled the control panel on the door. The forest canopy blocked much of the sunlight on this side as well, and dripped water on them as if it had recently rained. Monkeys chattered somewhere out of sight, and colorful birds flitted in and out of view.

"So, this is a rain forest," Quentin mused. "I've always wanted to see one in person."

"Haven't you ever watched the Discovery Channel?" Eissa asked. "You're liable to have a monkey humping your face before this is over, or get eaten down to the bone by army ants, or something. Everything in here will kill you."

Tocho laughed. "Well, it isn't quite as bad as all that."

He led them down a faint trail. It was covered in moss, as were the tree trunks and rocks. Even the vines hanging from the tree limbs had moss growing on them. The ferns and the moss were locked in fierce competition here, each trying to take over the world. Quentin shifted his backpack into a more comfortable position and jogged a few steps to catch up with Tocho and Eissa.

A few minutes later patches of blue sky began to appear, and suddenly they burst out of the forest and onto the shore of a large lake. To their left, fields of crops stretched into the distance. A mountain rose up on the far shore, its sides so steep that no trees grew there. Quentin's heart skipped a beat when he recognized what he had first mistaken for a cloud at the top as smoke.

"Is that an active volcano?" he whispered.

Tocho nodded, stopping to let them take in the magnificent view for a moment. "It sure is. Viho once told me it's been burning since before his father's father was a child."

The stunning contrast of the rain forest, the lake, the fields, and the volcano was mind-numbing. Four different worlds came together in a surreal overlap. Tocho turned and led them towards the fields.

"Somebody lives around here," Bob said. "I guess that's a good sign."

A trail led between the fields. On the right, corn towered overhead, tassels flapping in the breeze coming off the lake. Irrigation ditches surrounded the fields, with small wooden bridges where they crossed the trail. The field on the left was filled with vegetables and melons, each row different then the one beside it. They made their way down the trail, which had widened once they were across the first bridge and between the fields.

"Tak! Drahm tak! Ino bazda!"

Quentin froze at the sound of the shouting voice, his heart racing, and a moment later men with bows and arrows and cudgels came pouring out of the corn field, surrounding them. Quentin raised his hands overhead as one of them stepped forward, raising his cudgel with a fierce scowl. A slight moan escaped his lips, and he clamped down on it.

"Tak! Who are you? Who are these white people? Are you DimCorp?"

Eissa pressed up close against Quentin, her hands raised. He could feel her body shaking, and he turned his hip forward, sliding slightly in front of her. He couldn't do much to protect her from the warriors behind them, but taking some sort of action helped to curb his fear, however futile it might be. Tocho took a step forward, holding his hands out in front of him as if he were offering them a gift.

"My friends, I am Tocho, also called Straight Arrow. We are not DimCorp. We come to find the Bribri people."

The man in front lowered his stick a bit and glanced back at the others. Quentin realized they weren't really men at all, but rather teenage boys, some maybe in their early twenties.

They were shirtless and barefoot, wearing only shorts. Their brown skin was darker than Eissa's or Tocho's, and while they were certainly threatening with their long black hair and their weapons, they seemed more like farmers than warriors.

"I am Mazik," said the leader. He was more muscular than the others, with a bright pink scar on one cheek from the corner of his mouth all the way back to his ear. "I remember you. You came here when I was a boy." He turned back to the others and spoke in the unfamiliar language for a moment, and they lowered their weapons.

Quentin sagged as he lowered his arms, and let out a breath that he didn't remember holding. He didn't know if he would ever get used to people threatening him, but it hadn't happened yet. Bob heaved a sigh of relief behind Quentin and stepped around them. "Mazik, I'm Bob. I think I remember you, too. Isn't Viho your grandfather?"

Mazik nodded. The rest of his crew gathered in a loose knot behind him, and he turned to one. "Go tell the elders of this." The boy took off running down the trail.

"How is Viho?" Tocho asked. "Is he still the chief?"

Mazik nodded. "Yes. Come, we will go to the village and see him."

A ten-minute walk through the fields brought them to the edge of the village. There were cabins spread out across the meadow seemingly at random, with smoke curling from chimneys and chickens wandering around freely. The cabins were a combination of clay bricks and logs, with wood shingle roofs. Each cabin had a large garden surrounding it.

Mazik led them up the wide dirt path past the cabins to the central square. There were benches surrounding an open area, with a fire pit in the center. A small group of older men stood to one side waiting for them. As they approached, a stocky man with short gray hair stepped forward, his wrinkled, brown face lit up by a huge grin as he held out his arms.

"Tocho, my old friend!"

Tocho ran the last few steps and embraced him with a laugh.

"Viho, Viho, what's happened to the color of your hair? You became an old man."

"You don't look so young," Viho said, stepping back and looking Tocho up and down. "But then, you were old the last time I saw you, too."

They laughed together for a moment. Viho's eyes came to rest on Bob, and he stepped over.

"Bob, my old friend. What's going on? What brings you to our humble world after all this time?"

Bob hugged Viho and stepped back.

"Well, it's a complicated story. Let me introduce our friends, Quentin and Eissa, and maybe then we can sit down and talk."

"Of course, of course." Viho stepped over to Eissa and gave her a hug. "I am Viho, and you are welcome in my home."

He turned to Quentin and grasped his forearm in an iron grip. "I am Viho, and you are welcome in my home."

"Thank you, I'm Quentin." He tried to return the forearm grip, but he was caught at a bad angle, and couldn't do more than brush his fingers weakly against Viho's meaty arm. He managed an awkward smile as Viho released him and turned back to Eissa.

"You look more like Tocho and me than these other two. What people are you from?"

Eissa grinned. "I'm Chippewa, but I don't really know any other Chippewa people. I was adopted when I was a little kid."

Viho grinned, his eyes sparkling. "I haven't met any other Chippewa people either. Come, come, we will sit in my house and talk."

He led the way to a cabin on the other side of the square, scattering chickens as he went. As they climbed the steps to the porch, he held a bright orange curtain aside and gestured for them to enter. Quentin set his backpack down on the porch with the others beside a large loom and ducked through the low doorway into Viho's home.

The cabin was all one room, with lots of open windows letting in light and fresh air. Green and white curtains fluttered in the breeze, casting dancing shadows across the animal skins covering the floor. There was a small kitchen area with a fireplace to the left of the door, and sleeping pallets lined up along the back wall. To the right was an open area, with blankets and skins piled thick for seats.

The two elderly Bribri men that were with Viho moved to the middle of the seating area and sat down on the floor. Quentin sat down across from them, following their lead. As Eissa plopped down beside him, she ran her fingers through the hair on the white hide.

"This is ridiculously soft. I wonder what it is."

"Llama, from our friends in the south." Viho seated himself across from Quentin, completing the rough circle. "Those who came before our people had them here long ago, but now they only live in the high mountains with the Inka."

"Well, it's really nice," Eissa said.

Viho shifted his attention to Bob and Tocho as they were seated, and silence settled over the room.

"Where to start?" Tocho said. "How are things since Dim-Corp has been gone?"

The Bribri men glanced at one another, and the room became smaller and darker than it had been, making Quentin's skin crawl. Viho's voice was tightly controlled when he finally spoke. "DimCorp is not gone."

This time the stunned expressions belonged to Bob and Tocho, and Quentin realized with a sinking feeling that this was not going the way they expected it to.

"I don't understand," Bob said. "What happened? Did they come back?"

Viho shook his head and ran his thick fingers through his short grey hair. "They never left. We never got everyone out of the camp."

Tocho's eyes were wide, and his voice shook when he spoke. "Viho, I am sorry to hear this. We did not know."

"You couldn't know." He took a deep breath and blew it out. "I think of this every day, but it is still hard to speak of it." He stared hard at his hands for a moment, and then looked up at them. "When we rose up against Macalister and his men, we did what you taught us to do. We fought bravely, and four hundred of us made it out. Nearly one hundred died, and five hundred ended up staying there. Keme, my brother, looks after the ones who are still at the DimCorp camp."

Quentin whistled under his breath. "That's half the tribe."

Viho nodded. "Yes, we have been two tribes for five years now."

Silence settled over the room, heavy and still. The laughter of children playing drifted in the windows, but it sounded far away, and only made the silence more intense. Quentin cleared his throat.

"Well, that complicates things, huh?" He tried to smile, but a grimace was the best he could do. He looked at Viho and steeled himself. Everything was a training exercise, as Bob was fond of saying, and he was supposed to be developing his leadership skills, so this was the time for him to act the part he had been assigned. "I know you don't know me, Viho, but we came here to see if you and your people would teach us what you know about DimCorp, and how you fought them."

Viho stared at him, his wide brown face an expressionless mask. "What do you want to know?"

Eissa's hand found Quentin's and gave it a squeeze. It was a small thing, but it gave him the courage to keep going, and he plunged forward.

"Well, since it worked out the way it did, you probably have a good idea of what went right, and what went wrong. I guess that's a good place to start. I'd also ask you what you would do differently if you could do it all again."

Viho's eyes blazed. "If I could do it again, we would not do it. We would not fight."

"You'd keep the Bribri enslaved?" Quentin asked, puzzled. That wasn't the answer he'd been expecting at all. "Is that what you mean?"

"Easy, Quentin," Bob said in a hushed voice. "I'm sorry, Viho. Quentin's heart is in the right place, but he does not yet understand the pain involved in these things."

Viho stood and stalked over to the window. He brushed the curtain aside and stared outside mutely. Quentin silently berated himself for pushing too far, too fast. He should have waited and let Tocho and Bob run the conversation. How could he have failed to consider that this was deeply personal for Viho, and not just a conversation about an event? At last, Viho turned to face them.

"You want to know what I have learned? Here is what I learned. I have lived two lives. In the first life, my tribe was large. We were slaves, yes, and we worked hard, yes, and we were mistreated sometimes, yes. Understand this. My son was tall and strong, and he worked beside me. My people ate supper together at night, and we told stories to the children about the Goddess of the Mountain. We tended to the ones who were hurt that day, or sick. We were a tribe.

"In my second life, my tribe was small. We were free, yes, and we worked hard, yes, and no one mistreated us, yes, but understand this. My son was dead. Many people in my tribe were dead. Many of my tribe were still back at the DimCorp camp. And so, my heart was torn in three pieces. One piece was here, with the ones I still had. One piece was with the ones I left behind. One piece was with the dead. A heart torn three ways does not heal. It hurts every day when I wake up, and every night when I go to sleep."

He walked back over and sat down. "You ask me if I would keep my people slaves. I say I would keep my tribe together, I would keep my people alive. There are worse things than being a slave."

Quentin hung his head, shame burning his face. In all the training they had done over the last month, all the discussions about ethical principles, and theory of cause and effect, and dynamic impact, it had all been academic. He wasn't prepared for the human element. He had no way to speak intelligently to Viho, who had experienced both the processes and the emotional trauma of an uprising. The urge to get up and run back to the DimGate as fast as he could and escape to another dimension, any other dimension, was almost overpowering, and he had to channel his therapist to get through the moment. *Did you make a mistake, Quentin?* Yes. *Did anyone get hurt?* Viho's feelings were hurt. *Can you overcome this and move forward, or is it the end of the world?* I can overcome this. He took a shaky centering breath, and tried to come up with something to say, some meaningful response to Viho's powerful statement.

"Viho, I feel your pain," Eissa said softly. "I know what it's like to have people that you know and love dying all around you in battle. To wake up with an aching hole in your chest, because the person you used to eat breakfast with every day is dead, and you have to eat alone. It's a pain I still feel, too. You are not alone in this, and one thing I've learned is that having people who share your pain can lighten the weight of it."

Viho looked at Eissa with a flicker of gratitude in his eyes. Quentin realized that Eissa was able to connect with Viho in a way that he never could have, and he was glad that she had spoken up. Still, counseling Viho would only go so far. They had come here with the hopes of practicing a revolt, and learning the ropes, but these people clearly needed help. He couldn't bring back the dead, of course, but what if they could rescue the other half of the tribe, find a way to reunite them? That would do good, right?

A surge of hope shot through him at the idea, and he looked around the room. Bob and Tocho were staring at the floor, distress radiating from them in palpable waves. That was understandable. They were probably feeling responsible for all of this, and beating themselves up, instead of looking for solutions. Quentin almost chuckled at the reversal of roles.

Easy Q, don't get cocky. He took a deep breath to steady his nerves and stood up, clasping his hands to keep them from shaking.

"Viho, I'm sorry for the losses you have suffered. I'm sorry for the losses your people have suffered. I can't make that pain go away. However, the way I see it, we ought to be able to fix the other problem. If half your tribe is trapped in a plantation, then I think we should go get them out. Then your heart will only be torn in two, instead of three."

He held his breath as all eyes in the room turned to stare at him. He met their penetrating stares and tried to not look as scared as he felt.

"Whoa," Bob said, climbing slowly to his feet. "Hold on, let's don't go racing into that conversation. That's not what we came to do." He fixed an arresting stare on Quentin.

"Isn't it?" Quentin asked. The stab of humiliation he felt from the public rebuke was instantly replaced by anger. He knew he should keep his mouth shut, but he just couldn't do it. "We're supposed to be righting the wrongs of DimCorp, aren't we? It seems to me that we owe it to them to fix this. *You* owe it to them to fix this."

The challenge hung between them like a dark cloud. Bob's face turned purple, but Quentin was too angry to back down. He matched Bob's stare, daring him to deny responsibility. It was perfectly clear to Quentin that the only thing they could do now was what they had been training to do. There was no walking away. At last, Tocho stood and stepped between them, placing a hand on each of their shoulders.

"My friends, this is a very emotional moment. Before we say things we can't take back, let's stop and be silent. Listen to the wind, and let it cool your hearts."

Quentin looked away, his anger fading into righteous indignation. The room was deathly still, and the weight of their eyes on him was heavy. His limbs were leaden with adrenaline, and he allowed himself to sink back to the floor beside Eissa.

"Sorry, Bob," he mumbled.

Bob muttered something incoherent as he resumed his seat on the floor. Tocho closed his eyes and took a deep breath before also sitting down. The silence pressed in on Quentin, almost painfully, and he had to fight off another powerful urge to run away screaming. Slowly he became aware that the Bribri men were still in the room and had silently watched their argument. He risked a quick glance around.

The two older men sat impassively, their wooden faces displaying no emotion. In contrast, Viho stared at them incredulously. The stolid mask was slipping away from his face, and underneath it was a glimmer of emotion. Suddenly, he climbed back to his feet.

"I must get Tahki Ana."

He disappeared past the orange curtain in the doorway, and Quentin turned to Tocho with a questioning look, purposefully avoiding eye contact with Bob.

"She's the Matriarch," Tocho said. "Viho is the chief, but his wife is actually the leader of the tribe."

Quentin nodded mutely. He still wasn't sure if he had botched things with Viho, but he was positive he had botched things with Bob, and now it was escalating to another level. It was hard to say if that was good or bad. Viho was passionate, he was a tough, formidable guy, and intimidating as hell. What would his wife be like?

"I already like this place," Eissa said. "They let the men handle the petty stuff, and the women make the important decisions. That's my kind of tribe."

A few minutes later, Viho swept the door curtain aside. "Tahki Ana," he announced, stepping to the side and holding the curtain out of the way.

The Bribri men immediately stood, and Quentin scrambled to follow suit. His anger and shame were forgotten, trepidation taking their place. All eyes were on the door as Tahki Ana entered the room. Her simple blue shift hung loosely off her stocky frame, but her piercing dark eyes were like powerful magnets, and he was unable to look away from them.

Quentin immediately sensed her power. It wasn't that she was physically imposing, as she was at least a foot shorter than him. It was more like an electrically-charged aura that surrounded her, and it gave him a sense of confidence in her. There was absolutely no question about who was in charge. She embraced each of the Bribri men and murmured in their ears before turning to the visitors.

"Sit, please." She smiled at them. She sat in a beam of sunlight near the window, and the silver strands in her black hair glowed like bright flames. Quentin found himself mesmerized by her. "Tocho. Bob. It is with mixed feelings that I see you again."

Bob gave her a small smile, and looked at his feet, but Tocho held her gaze. "Tahki Ana. I understand your misgivings. I am sorry for the pain the Bribri have suffered because of us."

Her face softened. "You brought us ideas and hope, Tocho. We took the actions. You cannot carry all the blame." She glanced at Quentin and Eissa, then back to Tocho. "Viho tells me you want us to fight DimCorp again."

Before Tocho could respond, Quentin raised his hand. It wasn't fair for Tocho to have to defend his idea, or the fact that he had opened his mouth too soon.

Tahki Ana shifted her attention back to Quentin. "Who are you?"

"I'm Quentin James. I'm not really anybody important, but it was my idea to go rescue the rest of your people." He held her magnetic eyes and felt oddly strengthened by her confidence.

"And what is your plan? Tell me how you will bring my tribe back together without losing anyone else, and I will hear you."

Quentin took a deep meditative breath to still his heart. "We don't have a specific plan yet, as we don't know the situation. However, we want to achieve this in a non-violent way, so our intentions are in alignment with yours. We don't want anyone to die. If we can talk for a few minutes about what's going on at the plantation, then we will find a way to do this."

Tahki Ana stared deep into his eyes, and he willed himself not to wither under her intensity. He was dimly aware that there were others in the room, but it seemed that they had withdrawn into the shadows. He could feel her testing him, probing for any sign of disingenuity. *Be true to your personal mission, Quentin. Others will see your truth.*

"What do you need to know?" she asked at last. The light came back into the room, and Quentin pulled his eyes away from her for a moment and looked around.

"Well, so far we know that there are about five hundred Bribri in there, and that they're growing cacao. That's about all we've got. What else can you tell us? Do you have any contact with them at all?"

Viho pointed to Mazik. "My grandson sneaks in and carries news to my brother, Keme. We know most of what happens there."

Quentin nodded enthusiastically. "That's great, Mazik will be a huge resource. If we can coordinate with the people inside, that will make this much easier."

Viho grunted. "What has changed? Let's see. For a long time, the DimGate did not work, so they could not take the cacao to DimCorp. Macalister had them grow sugarcane and make chocolate, instead. He trades the chocolate to the Aztec and the Inka, and they give him food, gold, clothes, anything he wants. The DimGate works again though, we just learned this week."

"Do you know how many DimCorp people there are?"

Viho looked at Mazik and gestured for him to move forward. Mazik scooted up beside Bob. "Vincent Macalister and Morgan Gage, and thirty-nine guards."

Quentin looked at him in surprise. He had expected far more than that. Still, forty people with guns was a significant number. They weren't likely to let the Bribri walk away and just abandon the operation. If this was going to be a successful reuniting of the tribe, both the Bribri and DimCorp were going to have to work together and make some concessions. This was a strategy they had talked about ad nauseum back on the island, but sitting face-to-face with Viho and Tahki Ana, he was unsure that they would be receptive to the idea. He pushed forward, hoping he had enough momentum to carry him.

"I want to propose an idea. It's going to sound crazy at first, but please, hear me out." He looked at Viho, then fastened his eyes on Tahki Ana. Hers was the opinion that mattered the most. "DimCorp wants the cacao. Even if we get the Bribri out, DimCorp will come after you, or your neighbors. They will force someone to work the plantation, right? What about this? What if we went to the leader, what's his name?"

"Vincent Macalister," Viho said.

"Yes, Macalister. What if we went to Macalister and offered him a deal? If he's willing to improve the conditions and give the Bribri good housing with running water, and solar power, good food, real beds, that kind of stuff, and stop mistreating people, we will bring this half of the tribe back to the plantation to live and work as employees, instead of slaves."

Mazik shot to his feet, his face black with anger. "You are crazy! Why would we go back there? I will never do that."

Quentin recoiled from Mazik's hostility, his heart pounding.

"Mazik," Viho barked, pointing to the floor. Mazik clamped his mouth shut and sat, but the anger radiated from him in waves. Viho turned back to Quentin. "How would we hold him to that? Even if he accepted, and we went back, what would keep him from making it the way it used to be?"

"That's a fair question," Quentin said slowly. "For this, we would need to make a deal with the Aztec, or the Inka. The Bribri will be the workforce that supplies them with chocolate, or cacao, or whatever. That will keep DimCorp from coming to take them as slaves to replace the Bribri. That makes the Aztec safe from DimCorp, right? In return, if DimCorp reneges on their end of the deal, the Aztec army will come wipe out DimCorp. It's only forty guys, so they could do that easily. That's your security."

The room fell silent. Quentin prayed that he hadn't oversold the concept, or made it sound too easy. In truth, he had no idea if something like this would work or not. It was something that had come to him a few weeks before, and while they had tried to pick it apart and find all the flaws in the concept, they really hadn't expected to put it into action just yet. After all, this was supposed to be more training, not a real mission. And yet...

"If you walk into Macalister's office and offer him this, what security do you have?" Viho asked. "You don't know him. He's likely to make you a slave and put you to work. Why would he listen to you?"

"We have some bargaining power," Quentin said. "We're offering to double his workforce, and if he refuses, then we'll threaten to pull the Bribri out by force. I think he'll have to listen."

Viho chuckled without humor. "That is not enough. Macalister is brutal, and he will not be threatened so easily."

Quentin hoped that Bob or Tocho would chime in with some ideas. If Macalister was that tough, then what sort of leverage could they come up with to force him to negotiate? What would threaten him? A loss of workforce would get his attention, but they had already tried that once, and a hundred people had died. They would have to find a way to neutralize his strength, which was the forty guards. How would they do that?

"We need to find a way to get the guards out of the camp, and divide his forces," Quentin said slowly. "If we could lure them out a few at a time, and capture them, then we would have some leverage, right? How do we do that?"

He looked around the room. Viho's face was again an unreadable mask, but he could tell that Bob and Tocho were brainstorming. Bob was combing his beard with his fingers, which he took as an encouraging sign.

"You said they trade chocolate to the Inka and the Aztec, right?" Bob said, breaking the silence. Viho nodded. "What if we captured a trade convoy? We could get some of his guards that way, right?"

The idea began to grow the more Quentin thought about it. If they sent someone back to the plantation to tell them the trade convoy had been taken hostage, DimCorp would send more guards out to rescue them. That would weaken their forces inside the plantation significantly, and perhaps give them the leverage they needed to force Macalister to listen to them.

"I think that's the answer," Quentin said. "We can probably get half their guys outside the camp like that."

Tahki Ana shifted slightly, and a hush fell over the room as she looked at them. "If we do this, we risk the lives of our young men, like Mazik."

"I will fight DimCorp," Mazik declared. "I am not afraid." His face darkened as he thrust his chin up in defiance, the scar on his cheek becoming even more pronounced.

"Yes, Mazik, I know that you will fight." Tahki smiled sadly. "And what would you have me tell your mother? That to lose her husband to DimCorp was not enough? That she must sacrifice her son, too, as I sacrificed mine?"

The words hung in the air. Mazik said nothing, but his posture remained rigid as she continued.

"If we don't do this, then half our people will live the rest of their lives in bondage. The children will grow up with the scars of whips upon their backs, and we will grow old with those scars upon our hearts. It is not so easy to walk back into the house of Vincent Macalister and tell him we want to come do his work, even for the rewards you have talked about.

It is not so easy to capture his guards, either. People will be hurt and killed. But I also see the future, and that is not so easy to accept."

She looked at each of them in turn, her eyes coming to a stop on Bob. "You bring death, Bob, everywhere you go, even with your good intentions. My heart is heavy with grief even before it begins." She stood, and kept them seated with a wave of her hand. "Make your preparations. You have everything we have to offer. I hope it is worth the price we will pay."

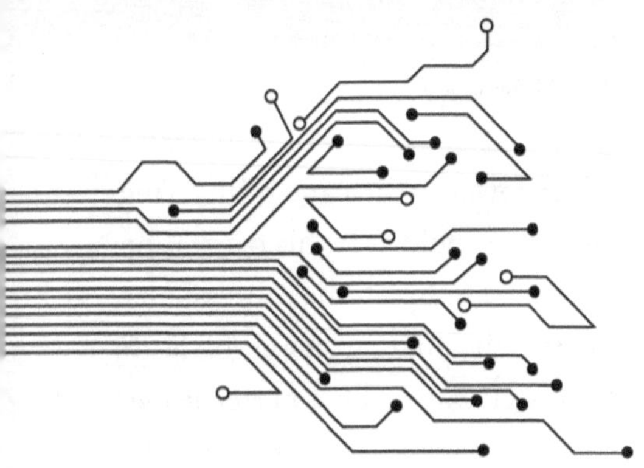

CHAPTER 4

Morgan Gage closed the door to Macalister's office, walked down the short, dim hall, and stepped out onto the porch into the sunlight. He swallowed his rage, and made sure that his face was impassive as he walked past the ever-present Bader, who was in his usual spot on the porch.

There was no reason for any of this to be so stressful. If Macalister would show him the slightest bit of respect and treat him with dignity, they could be a great team. The hell of it was, Macalister couldn't see what an asset he had in Gage. He had been third in his class at the DimCorp Leadership Academy. He had helped mediate and resolve a major worker's rebellion at a diamond mine in another dimension during his internship. He was smart, and he was committed. Why wouldn't Macalister be happy to have him on the team?

He clearly wasn't, though, and he made no effort to disguise his distaste for Gage's style and ideas. That was one thing, but this insistence on keeping the chocolate business going when Headquarters said no was something else altogether. Forcing him to send a runner to the Inka was a total dick move. Macalister was trying to make him look like an asshole to the workers. Nobody was going to volunteer to deliver that message. It was a suicide mission.

He walked down the street towards the cane mill, trying to push the rage out of his mind. He couldn't let his frustration show to the guards or the workers. He had to be professional, detached, and composed. It was the first principle of leadership. The way to beat Macalister was to be a better leader than him, and that was something he could do with ease. Still, it would be nice if he could talk to someone about this stuff, perhaps one of his mentors from school. It was hard being isolated out here.

The idea of the gold was tantalizing, but he had conflicting feelings about it. At the Academy, they had taught that this sort of thing was never acceptable, but Macalister's explanation of fringe perks made sense. He was young, but not too young to know that sometimes corporate policy said one thing, and best practices said something else. It was doubtful that Macalister would give him much of it anyway, but still. Maybe he could do something about that. It would be nice to have his own nest egg. He could probably skim some of the gold off the shipments before they ever got back to camp. That was one thing that befriending the guards and workers gave him that Macalister would never get from them: favors. The guys on the trade convoys would probably do it just to stick it to Macalister.

In the four years since Morgan Gage had been assigned to this project, Macalister had moved steadily further and further away from the corporate plan. It had been small steps at first, but once the DimGate shut down and stayed down, he had quickly gotten bolder. Gage had been helpless to do anything but watch as Macalister became a tyrant.

When he got to the mill, he found that work had stopped. Several guards stood around the area, along with the workers. Keme, the head foreman of the workers, was taking the screws out of the cover for the gear casing, handing them to a child who stood beside him with a bucket of tools.

"Did the mill go down?" Gage asked, working his way to the front.

"Yes, boss, the shear pin, probably," Keme said, glancing over at him. "I'll know in a minute."

"Alright, the rest of you go help out the juice crew. We can't have everyone standing around."

He stepped up beside Keme and helped him lift the heavy cover plate off the mill and set it down. He pulled a flashlight out of the bucket and shined it down inside the gear housing. It was dark and dirty inside. The mill was a simple design, one that had been in use forever. A 20-foot-long horizontal handle was attached to a vertical center shaft that stuck out the top of the mill housing. The workers walked in a circle around the mill, pushing the handle. This turned the shaft, which turned gears inside. The grinder was attached to one side, and it was just two wide cylindrical gears that turned in on each other as the handle was pushed. A worker fed the sugar cane into the gears which crushed it, squeezing out the juice which ran to a collection vat.

"Looks like a rock in the crusher," Keme said. "That'll do it every time."

Gage moved the light over the gears to the base of the vertical shaft. Just above the gears at the base, the upper shaft slid over the lower shaft, with a bolt going through the center of them to hold them together. This was the designed fail point, so that the crusher wouldn't be damaged if a rock or something made its way into the gears. The bolt had been sheared off, as it was supposed to do in such a situation.

"Alright, let's get it changed out. Do we have any shear pins left?"

"We've got one left, boss." Keme rummaged around in the bucket and pulled out a punch and a short-handled sledge hammer. "That needs to be on the first requisition order we put in. Can't do much without them."

"I know," Gage said. He grabbed the punch from Keme. "I'll hold the punch and the flashlight, you drive it out."

Keme looked at him for a moment and nodded. "Alright."

This was a trust-building technique that Gage liked to use, but it was hard to find opportunities to do it. Macalister was violently opposed to the whole concept and had reamed him out over it more than once. *Are you crazy, giving a slave the opportunity to hurt you?* Macalister had shouted at him. *I'm showing the workers that I trust them, and they can trust me,* he had responded. It had fallen on deaf ears.

He held the punch up to the bolt hole and shined the light on it. Keme repositioned slightly and gave the punch a test tap with the hammer.

"Alright boss, you ready?"

Gage nodded.

Keme swung the sledge hammer. It landed with a solid impact on the punch, sending a vibration up Gage's arm to his elbow. He gritted his teeth and tried to hold the light still as Keme swung again. It took five swings to knock the bolt out the back side of the hole, and by the time it broke free, Gage's arm was screaming in protest to the jarring blows. He dropped the punch in the bucket and grinned at Keme as he massaged his wrist.

"One of these days I'm going to learn to let somebody else hold the punch. That kills my arm every time."

Keme chuckled. "I would have traded places with you, boss, but I've seen you swing a hammer before."

Gage laughed. "Come on, man, I'm not that bad."

Keme removed the broken shear pin pieces and the rock from the gears. Gage tapped the new pin in, and together they lifted the cover back in place. As they started the screws, Gage steeled himself for the difficult conversation that he had been leading up to. He glanced around, making sure no one else was in earshot.

"I need a runner to send to the Inka. It's not going to go very well. Who do you have that can take a tough message?"

Keme stopped turning the wrench and tensed up, staring fixedly at the bolt. "What kind of tough message?"

Part of him wanted to rebel against Vincent Macalister, to ignore the order and not send a runner. Standing in front of Keme, it seemed like the right thing to do, but it would be a different story when he was standing back in front of Macalister. He hated being in this position. It was the very worst part of leadership.

"Macalister wants to change the deal. No more food, no more clothes, just gold. And the price is going up."

Keme turned slowly to face him. "You know the man that takes that message in there isn't coming back. It's a death sentence."

Gage held his eyes, trying to keep the guilt he felt off his face. Of course he knew he was sending someone to die. That's why his stomach was churning, making him feel like he might have to race for the outhouse any second. Macalister knew it too, and that's why he was making Gage deliver the order. He was such a vindictive bastard. Gage took a deep breath and let it out slowly.

"Look, Keme, I don't like this any more than you do. Hell, I tried to explain to him that we need the food a lot more than he realizes, but he wasn't hearing it. You know how he gets."

Keme's lips trembled, and his eyes grew dark. "You talk to me about your beliefs, about how you want to change things for the Bribri, and then you come to me with this? How long until you stop talking and take a stand against him? How many boys like Charto, there, have to get hurt or killed until you decide it's time to stand up to him?"

"What do you want me to do?" Gage asked, his eyes blazing. "I have to go through the proper channels to get him replaced, and that takes time. This is now. I can't stall this for a month while I'm waiting on a chance to file a complaint with his supervisor. I don't have any choice."

Keme turned away. He was at the breaking point, and clearly anything Gage tried to say now would be wasted. This wasn't how he wanted the conversation to go. Keme was bright, and he was a good leader. He had to understand the position Gage was in. Yes, he had promised Keme that if he could get Macalister removed from his position, that they would work together to make life better for the workers. He stood by that promise, but it wasn't something that was going to happen overnight. The DimGate had only been functioning for a few weeks, and it wasn't like he could just run over to the Genesis Dimension and fill out a complaint form on his lunch break.

Maybe they could change up the messenger, send someone that the Inka wouldn't kill. What if they sent a woman? Women were revered in the Bribri tribe, but the Inka didn't have the same system. They would probably keep her as a slave. A child? That wouldn't go much better. They'd be suspicious of a runner that wasn't a man or a boy and disregard the message anyway. Not that Keme would send a woman; he would probably go himself before doing that.

Frustration boiled up inside Gage and he gave into it. He turned towards the nearby hut where the juice crew was working.

"Charto, come here. Now."

Charto dropped the firewood he was carrying and ran over. He was a thin boy, maybe twelve or thirteen, with a dirty face, but his eyes were bright. He smiled at Gage as he skidded to a stop.

"Yes, boss?"

"Go pack some food. I need you to take a message to the Inka." He looked over at Keme. His pulse was pounding in his temple and his mouth was dry. He had lost his temper, and that made him even more angry. "Keme will tell you what to say to the Inka. Go get your stuff."

Charto ran off.

He wanted to lash out at Keme for making him feel like such a heartless bastard, but he knew it was really Macalister who was doing that to him. Keme was just a victim of circumstance, like himself. Well, that wasn't fair. After all, Keme was a worker. A slave. He didn't like to use that word, but it helped him divert his anger. Keme was a slave, and he couldn't be mad at the slave for resenting the master. A master that made him sacrifice one of his own, no less. His anger dissipated, leaving him feeling empty and dirty.

Keme turned back to the cover and began tightening the screws, his jaw clenched. Gage felt like throwing up. He wanted to apologize to Keme, but there were no words, so he turned away and walked down the road towards the fields. He needed some time alone to figure out a plan. Clearly, he had to do something about Macalister. He just didn't know what, or how.

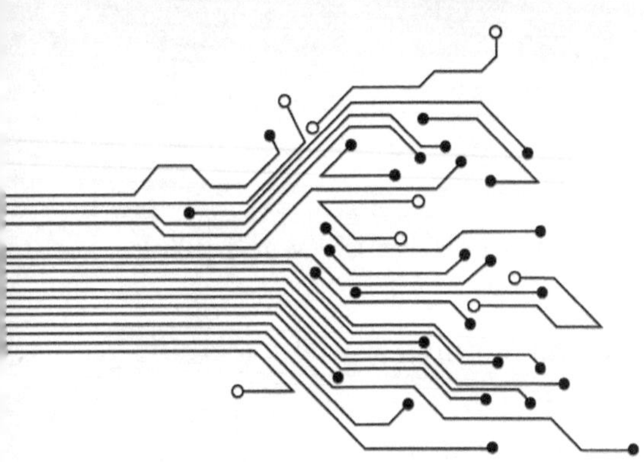

CHAPTER 5

Vincent Macalister walked out onto the porch and looked around the compound. To his left, Bader was seated in his usual spot, guarding the door. Across the courtyard, the guards were gathering up for the midday meal outside the mess hall. The sound of laughter and boasting drifted across the muddy expanse. To his right, down past the warehouse, the slaves were seated on the ground in front of the sugarcane processing hut, eating their lunch. A few guards lounged nearby, and he knew there were more on the other side, out of view. He turned back to the guards at the mess hall, and looked at his watch.

"A little early for lunch, isn't it?" He spoke loudly, his voice echoing off the rear wall of the warehouse that spanned the gap between them.

The laughter and grab-assing stopped instantly, and a small grin tugged at the corner of his lips as they cringed and turned towards him. That was control, man, that was *power*. It was almost as intoxicating as the gold. Almost. He looked at his watch again.

"It looks to me like everybody over there owes me ten minutes at five o'clock. Is that what it looks like to you?"

"Yes, boss." The low chorus lacked the enthusiasm he would have preferred, but he decided he didn't feel like pushing it.

"Bader."

"Yes, boss." The legs of the chair hit the wood plank floor with a bang as Bader leaned forward and stood up.

"It's been a rough goddamn morning. I need something to cheer me up."

"You want me to bring you a woman?"

He briefly considered it, but not too seriously. Fucking the slave girls while he was in a bad mood wasn't a good idea. He'd done it before, of course, but he had a tendency to knock them around when he was angry, and the one time he'd actually killed one of them, they'd almost had another revolt on their hands. That kind of thing slowed down production for weeks, and it just wasn't worth it. Best to wait until he felt better about things.

"Nah, it's too hot for that shit. Let's take a walk."

"I'm with you, boss."

Good old Bader. Dumb as a fucking rock, but loyal to the death, and willing to fight anyone Macalister pointed him towards. He walked down the steps, with Bader right behind him.

Halfway down the side of the warehouse, he stopped and opened a door. The inside of the warehouse was dim, lit only by the skylights overhead. This side was where the dried cacao nibs were stored. To Macalister, they smelled like mushrooms, musty and faint, but in a good way. He breathed deeply as they walked down the aisle to the back, relishing the moment. In here, there were no employees, no slaves, no DimCorp, no problems. This was his go-to corner, and he guarded it jealously.

At the end of the row was another door. This one had a padlock on it, and a deadbolt just below it. Macalister had a key to one, and Bader had a key to the other. For someone to get both keys would be impossible without killing them both, and that was very unlikely. Macalister motioned Bader to the padlock.

"You'd better have your key."

"Sure do, boss." Bader reached inside his collar and produced the key, which hung around his neck on a rawhide cord. He opened the padlock as Macalister unlocked the deadbolt, and they went inside.

Macalister waved his hand over his head in the darkness, and eventually found the string hanging. He gave it a tug, and the bright LED bulb came to life. He stood with his back to the door, knowing that the first thing he would see when the light came on was the goblet. As the shadows retreated, his heart began to pound, as it always did when he saw it. Out of all the wonderful things made of gold in this room, this was his favorite. He picked it up with a loving smile.

It was a massive solid gold goblet, with a solitary ruby set in the side of it. It was ridiculously heavy, and would probably be awkward to drink from, but he loved it. Holding it made him feel superior to everyone else. If someone saw him at a party holding the goblet filled with wine, they would know that he was someone important. This goblet told everyone who the motherfucker-in-charge was. He set it back down and carefully wiped it off with a handkerchief.

He wandered down the line. There were piles of arm bands. Some were plain, and some were engraved with tribal artwork. There were trinkets in the shapes of various animals, more than a few idols of outlandish figures, and even a large plate with a battle scene engraved on it. Most of it was meaningless to him, at least in terms of art. Aside from the goblet, the rest of it was just gold, money. It represented a way out of this shitty dimension.

"You feeling any better, boss?" Bader asked from the doorway.

He took a deep breath, and slowly blew it out his nose, relaxing. "Yeah, man, I'm getting there."

"That's good, boss, that's good."

This room was another improvement he hadn't mentioned to the corporate monkey. They'd be sure to give him hell about relocating lights and solar panels from staff quarters, and he didn't want to hear that shit. At this point, he needed to empty the room anyway, and they could have their lights back after that. First, he needed to figure out what to do with all this stuff.

"I'm thinking about melting all this down and pouring it into bars so it doesn't take up so much space. What do we have that we could use as a mold?"

Bader's forehead scrunched up, giving him a dark, bushy unibrow. "That's a tough one, boss. I don't think we really got anything that wouldn't burn up."

Macalister looked away to hide a smile. Bader was the only person in the camp that he tried to avoid insulting, at least most of the time.

"Well, keep your eyes open. If you run across something, let me know. We gotta get this stuff out of here pretty quick."

"I'm on it, boss."

"One other thing." Macalister looked back at him to make sure he had his complete attention. "I want you to keep an eye on Gage for me. He's starting to buck me. I want to know what he's telling the boys behind my back."

Bader nodded eagerly. "You got it, boss."

Once again, Macalister thought about having Bader kill Gage. He'd thought about it before, of course, hundreds of times, and while he always came to the same conclusion, he couldn't let the idea go completely. Especially now, with Corporate becoming a part of things again. Why couldn't the damn DimGate have stayed down another year or two? That would have made things so much easier. He could have stockpiled twice as much gold, gotten Gage out of the picture, and retired like a king. He still could, but Gage could screw that up for him, too. He was just too much of a rule-follower, a company man. He was such a tight-ass that he might not even accept the idea of taking gold as a perk. Macalister shook his head. How do you reason with somebody that can't think for himself?

Bader, now there was a guy he might be willing to share the gold with. If anyone had earned a piece of it, it was him. He'd been loyal right from day one, and never questioned anything Macalister told him to do. Hell, he might even take Bader with him when he retired. He'd be useful to have around, especially with all the gold. When you were rich like that, you needed some reliable muscle to protect you.

"What do you think about retiring to the Caribbean, Bader?"

"Boss?"

Macalister tossed him a gold armband. "I'm talking about you and me getting the fuck out of this miserable goddamn place. We could go back to the Genesis Dimension, cash this in at a gold dealer, and go live in some exotic dimension. Every day, sitting on a beach, rum and pussy everywhere."

Bader grinned shyly, looking down at the armband in his hands. "Sounds good, boss. Sounds real good."

Macalister nodded absently. He couldn't just walk away, of course. DimCorp was going to have to be dealt with, but that was paperwork. It could be handled. Grease a few palms here and there to speed up the process, and he could be out of here in less than a year. He could do anything for a year, if there were millions of dollars waiting on the other end of it. The only potential problem was Gage.

"You keep your nose glued to Gage. We can't let him fuck this up for us, right? I've busted my ass to make this happen. If he rats us out to Corporate about this gold, we're both fucked, and I'm not about to let that happen. If he says a prayer, I want to know what he asks for. If he sends a letter to his mother, I want to know how many x's and o's he puts on the bottom of it, you hear me?"

"I hear you, boss."

"Don't be obvious about it, either. Use your little team, if you're sure they can be trusted. If you've got doubts about their loyalty, don't say shit to them. This is totally off the radar, got it?"

"I got it," Bader said. "Incognito."

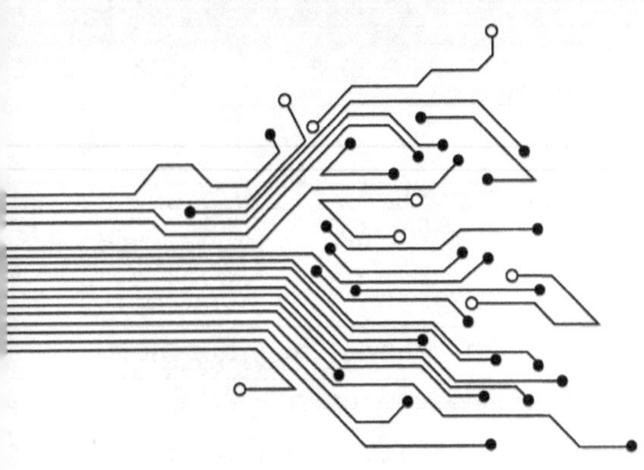

CHAPTER 6

"**S**o, how many people do we have to work with here?" Quentin asked. "People that can fight, let's start with that." They were back in Viho's house for a brainstorming session after taking a break to explore the village and cool off.

Viho nodded. "We have almost five hundred people. Out of that, about one hundred fifty are children, too small. Our women are tough, but they are not warriors, and that's about two hundred. So, one hundred fifty men. Some of them are too old to fight. About one hundred who can run, and use a bow or a spear."

"Okay, that's not so bad," Quentin said. "If Macalister has a total of forty men, then we outnumber him significantly."

Quentin was back in charge of planning, after a heated discussion with Bob and Tocho. Quentin wanted to take a giant step back after the debacle at the first meeting and learn from the sidelines, but they weren't having it. They'd promised to support him, but he was running the show.

"Don't forget that they have guns," Bob said. "Bullets against arrows are a great equalizer."

"Maybe," Quentin said. "Maybe not. In our dimension, General Custer and his army with guns got the shit kicked out of them by the Indians. No survivors."

"Native Americans," Eissa corrected. "And I think they had guns, too."

Quentin sighed, trying not to get annoyed. "Some of them might have, but not all of them. Anyway, that's not the point. We're not trying to kill anyone, remember?"

Eissa stuck her tongue out at him. Her refusal to take things seriously was a survival mechanism, part of her PTSD, but knowing that didn't make it any less irritating for him. He was trying desperately to look professional in front of the Bribri, and her immature behavior made him feel like a little kid playing dress-up in front of the grown-ups. He shifted away from her slightly, as if the increased gap between them would separate her behavior from his in the eyes of the others.

"What's your idea?" Bob asked. "I can see the gears turning in your head."

"Well, it's just a rough idea," Quentin said slowly. "If we ambush one of his chocolate trade groups, or convoy, whatever you call it, like you had mentioned, and we manage to keep the element of surprise, we should be able to capture the lot without a single shot fired. It's not like they'll be marching down the road with their guns drawn, right? They do this all the time; they're not expecting trouble."

"Right," Bob agreed.

"So, if a hundred guys jump out of the woods with arrows drawn, surrounding them, they can't do anything. We'll totally have the drop on them. Then we just disarm them, tie up the guards, release the slaves, and job done."

Quentin looked around the group, hoping for some glimmer of support. Mazik spoke up.

"If we have them like that, why don't we just shoot them

all? Three seconds, a hundred arrows, and it's all over. Then they don't have a chance to shoot anyone."

"Well, that hurts our chances of making a deal with Macalister," Quentin pointed out. "We can't kill all of his men, and then ask him to meet us in the middle." He didn't add that killing people wasn't on his skills list.

"If we kill all his men, and kill him too, then we can just take over the chocolate trade," Mazik said with a dark smile. "We'll make our own deal with the Inka and the Aztecs."

Quentin took a deep breath. He wasn't a natural diplomat, and he certainly wasn't prepared to spend the day talking someone out of going on a killing rampage. The whole discussion with Viho and Tahki Ana had been geared towards *not* getting anyone hurt or killed. Mazik was clearly on a different sheet of music than his grandparents.

Tocho cleared his throat. "If we kill everyone, then we become bad people, just like DimCorp. We are the good guys. We don't want to kill anyone, if we can help it."

"They are soldiers," Mazik said. "Killing them is not the same as killing other people."

The concept of nonviolence seemed to be lost on Mazik. If they couldn't trust him to not start shooting arrows into the DimCorp guards, then they were going to have a serious problem. He needed to find a way to help Mazik broaden his perspective and see the bigger picture. Quentin tried to come up with a commonality between Mazik and the guards. If he could plant that seed, perhaps he could coax some empathy out of it.

"They're people," Quentin said. "They have hopes and dreams and families, just like you and me. They have values, just like we do. Theirs might be different than ours, but we have to be true to our values, and killing them, especially from ambush when they're defenseless, is wrong."

Mazik glared at Quentin, anger clouding his eyes like a storm, and pointed to the scar on his cheek. "Do you think the man who did this was worried about my hopes and dreams and family? He killed my father with the same knife that gave me this scar. He deserves to die."

Viho raised his hand, silencing the room. He bowed his head for a moment.

"Mazik is young, and he has suffered much," he said. "He does not yet understand that you cannot bring peace to the world by killing all of your enemies."

The first thing Quentin's therapist would ask is if he had tried to see things from Mazik's perspective. If his own father had been killed by Carl Holt, the DimCorp security guard that had started Quentin down this path, would he be able to set that aside and be pragmatic? It was easy to say that he would, in a theoretical sense, but he couldn't deny that he would want justice, and if he couldn't get that, then he would settle for vengeance. Hell, if he was being honest with himself, he had to admit that he'd acted just like Mazik only a month ago, when he was more concerned about going home and confronting Carl Holt and Gerrard Zimmerman than he was about confronting DimCorp as a whole.

There was a lot more pain and suffering in Mazik's past than Quentin gave him credit for, and he felt guilty for not acknowledging that beforehand. If he was going to guide Mazik effectively, he had better understand what motivated Mazik. Logic wasn't going to be enough, by itself. He needed to speak to Mazik's pain points.

"If we kill forty men from DimCorp, four hundred will

come through the Gate," Quentin said. "If we kill them, four thousand will come. It is without end."

Mazik was silent, brooding.

"The way forward is not through killing," Viho said. "If killing were the answer, then there would only be one man left in the world, and he would die alone, with no one to care that he ever lived."

Mazik hung his head. "Yes, grandfather."

Quentin was taken aback by Viho's nugget of wisdom. He hadn't really thought about it like that before, but it was hard to argue with. If he killed everyone he disagreed with, he would have already killed everyone in this room at least once. The concept chilled him.

Viho turned to Quentin. "This ambush, what happens if a guard shoots his gun?"

"Well, we have to defend ourselves. If someone starts shooting, then kill him, but only him. There must be discipline to not start killing the others, too."

Viho nodded in silence.

"I think we need to see what we've got for resources," Bob said. "If we go with this plan, we're going to need a lot of rope to tie up the guards."

"We have rope as well as rawhide," Viho said. "We'll soak it and cut it into strips. We use that to tie many things. It is very strong."

Bob nodded and ran his fingers through his beard.

"Okay, let's plot this out," Quentin said. He leaned forward and drew a line across the llama skin with his finger. "That's the trail. How many people are going to be in the trade group? Has anyone ever seen how they do it?"

"Two guards lead the way," Mazik said. "Then come five

Bribri, with packs. Three guards behind them, and five more Bribri. Five guards at the end."

If the trade convoy was really that small, walking down a trail in dense jungle foliage, an ambush with a hundred people wasn't going to be practical at all. He was going to have to scale it back, but that might be a good thing. If he could split his forces in half, they could do a lot more.

"Okay, so we're looking at ten guards, spaced out along here." Quentin pointed to the line. "If we have twenty men with bows, we can put ten on each side. Every man is assigned to a guard. Bob and I step out on the trail and stop them and tell them they're surrounded. If a guard starts to raise his gun, the two men assigned to him shoot him. No one else shoots. Then ten other men come up and disarm the guards and tie them up. What do you think?"

"Why not have fifty on each side?" Eissa asked. "Overwhelm them with numbers."

"It's going to be hard enough to hide twenty people where they can't be seen easily, but still have a clear shot," Quentin said. "I don't think you could hide a hundred people in the woods and keep them close enough to the trail to be effective."

"Fair point," she said. "So, where am I in all of this?"

"You're the medic, so we need to find a spot that's close to set you up with the medical gear. If someone does get hurt, we need to be able to get them to you pretty quick."

Eissa smiled, as he knew she would. Once she had a purpose, a direction, she would fully engage with it, and he wouldn't have to worry about it. That was doubly true with a first aid station. Give Eissa a medical mission, and she was in her element.

"Do you want me to be mobile and come to you, or do you want me to have a spot where I set up a triage center, and you bring them to me?"

"What is happening?" Viho asked. "What is a triage center?"

"It's basically a field hospital," Eissa said. "I brought a lot of medical supplies so we could practice realistically, which was a good decision, as it turns out. Hopefully we won't need them, of course."

"Are you a doctor?" Mazik asked, perking up. "When I was a boy, a DimCorp doctor came through the Gate and healed a guard who broke his leg."

Eissa shook her head. "No, I was a combat medic. My job in the Army was to keep people alive long enough to get them to a doctor."

"A triage center is probably the best way to do it," Quentin said, trying to get them back on topic. "If you're mobile, we'll have to have people carrying gear for you, and digging around trying to find what you need, and all that."

He turned to Viho.

"We don't want anyone to get hurt, but if they do, we want to be ready to help them as best we can. Do you have someone that can help her, someone with experience like this?"

"Yes, of course," Viho said. "We have three women who will help her. They are very good healers."

Quentin consulted his list. They were doing a fairly good job of covering the bases. They didn't have a second plan to compare it to, or at least not yet, and that was something he wanted to move on to soon. He was already learning that there was a lot he didn't know about doing something like this, and the last thing he wanted was for his lack of experience to get someone hurt or killed.

"Bob, what do you think about this plan?" Quentin asked. "You're the one with all the experience. How can we do it better?"

Bob looked at Tocho before answering. Tocho shrugged.

"Well, it's basically the same concept I had," Bob said. "We've used something similar before. The biggest flaw I see is that you're pretty sure they're just going to drop their guns and surrender. I guess that's possible, but usually there's at least a couple that want to shoot it out. You have to be prepared for that."

Logically, no one should try to shoot it out when they're surrounded, and it was a good reminder that people are seldom logical, especially in an emotionally-charged situation. It was difficult for Quentin to anticipate things like this, and he nodded to Bob in gratitude.

"I'm hoping to talk them out of that," Quentin said. "Maybe you and I can step out and talk to them. We'll tell them that we don't want anyone to get hurt, but they're surrounded by archers who will shoot them if they move their hands. That way, they'll have a second to think it through. Obviously, we don't want everyone jumping up and pointing bows and arrows at them. I don't want to make it a race thing, but I think they'll listen to us since we're white."

"What the fuck is that supposed to mean?" Eissa asked. Her face darkened into a frown.

"It means that they aren't expecting any white people to be there." Quentin swallowed his frustration, determined not to get lured into an argument with her in the middle of a strategy meeting. "If the Bribri just pop up, they'll assume they're being robbed, and probably start shooting. If two white guys appear and want to talk, they'll be confused enough to hear us out."

Eissa held his stare for a moment, her jaw clenched. He could tell that she knew he was right from the twitch in her eye, but that she hated to admit it. It was an understandable sticking point for her, but he needed her to get past it.

"It is wise to play on the prejudices of your enemy," Tocho said. "Bob and I used that strategy for many years."

"Well, I guess that makes sense," Eissa said, dropping her eyes at last. "But you sounded like an asshole when you said it."

"I'm sorry. I'll work on my presentation." Quentin winked at her as a way of apologizing. She gave him a small smile.

"You know that by doing that, you're making yourself an easy target," Bob said. "There's nowhere for us to hide if it goes bad."

"Well, how else can we do it?" Quentin asked. "That's the kind of feedback I need here. What can we do to make it safer, more foolproof?"

No one said anything. Quentin went over the diagram, trying to improve on it, but there were only three moving pieces, and he couldn't come up with another way to reach the desired conclusion. When the trade convoy came down the trail, they needed to be stopped, notified of the situation, and disarmed and restrained. There just wasn't another way to accomplish that.

"Well then, I guess that's Plan A," Quentin said. "If it works, then we send one of the pack carriers back to the camp to tell them they got attacked, and we do it again on the second set of guards that shows up."

He looked around the room. Viho sat silently, his stone face unmoving. Mazik's eyes glittered, and his agitated fingers drew patterns on the llama skin. The contrast between the two was striking; the stillness of experience and wisdom, and the energy of righteous rage.

"The second group of guards is going to show up ready for war," Bob said. "If they think there's a battle going on, they're liable to shoot first and ask questions later, as the saying goes. We'll have to figure out how to de-escalate things, so it doesn't turn into a blood bath."

There didn't seem to be any way to handle them differently than the first group. There were the same three moving parts. The only way to approach it was for someone to approach them with a white flag and try to talk it out. He couldn't argue with Bob about the danger in that. The very thought of standing alone with his hands raised over his head as a group of men with machine guns raced towards him made his bowels loose with fear, but what else could he do? There was no other way.

"I have a bad feeling," Viho said. "I remember everything that has been said, but I do not like any of this. I wish now that you had not come."

"That wouldn't have stopped the future from happening," Bob said. "Half your tribe would still be slaves. Eventually, DimCorp would want more. They will always want more slaves to take more resources, until they have taken everything in your land. And if it's not them, then someone else from this world would show up one day and try to take it away from you."

A breeze picked up the curtains and waved them about, their shadows dancing across the floor. Dust motes floated in the sunbeams, stirred by the moving air. The silence was heavy, but less pressing than before.

"Are all men so greedy in their heart?" Viho asked. "Is no people safe in their own land?"

"Not really," Quentin said. "They call it colonizing, or empire-building. People have been doing it to each other forever. Some people want things, and the way they get it is by finding people like the Bribri and taking it from them. Sometimes it's land, sometimes it's labor, or gold, or oil. They move in, take over, and get what they want. Eventually, someone else will come along and do the same thing to them."

Viho shook his head, and Quentin realized he was crying. He reached over and put his hand on Viho's shoulder and squeezed.

"We think it's horrible, too. That's why we're here. We're trying to fight back."

Viho put his hand on top of Quentin's.

"I know this," he said. His voice shook with emotion as he looked at each of them in turn. "The sadness is heavy on my heart when I think about all of my people who have died for this already. My son. The sons of my friends and family. What have they died for? For a cacao seed? Is that the value of life to these people? I would have given them a thousand bushels of seeds if they had asked. Instead, the Bribri people died, and became slaves... for nothing. This is my sadness."

Quentin's chest tightened. He was powerless to stop the grief that radiated from Viho, and it poured over him in relentless waves. He pushed the emotions down and tried to compartmentalize them, to seal them off, at least until the meeting was over. If he started crying too, he might not be able to stop.

They sat in silence for several minutes, contemplating Viho's words. Quentin used the time to slow his pounding heart and get refocused on the logistics of the situation. *Gotta stay logical, Q. Don't be an emotional sponge.* Sometimes it was helpful to be empathic and feel the emotions of those around you. In this situation, though, where there was such an overwhelming volume of powerful emotions, it would drown him if he let it. He knew what they were feeling, he didn't need to feel it with them. Best to put the emotions in a box and lock the lid. When he felt that it was safe to resume the discussion, he cleared his throat lightly.

"We need to know the layout of the camp, too," he said. "I think we've done the best we can with getting most of the guards out. What do we do after that? How hard is it to get into the camp?"

"It has a wall all the way around it," Mazik said. "It goes around the cacao groves, all the way to the river. There is a gate, that is how they get out, but it has guards."

"Well, it sounds like we go through the gate," Bob said.

"Wait," Quentin said. "Mazik, how do you get in when you go talk to your uncle?"

"I sneak in through the river," Mazik said. "At night, I swim out around the fence and go in through the cacao grove to take messages to Keme."

"Are there guards at the river?" Tocho asked.

Mazik shook his head. "No, the river has crocodiles and caribes. They don't expect anyone to come in that way."

"What's a caribe?" Quentin asked.

"Small fish with many teeth," Mazik said. "They are very bad."

"Oh, like piranha," Eissa said. "Well, that's a fair

assumption. That's enough to keep me out of the river."

Crocodiles and caribes probably provided better security than the guards could. It was enough to keep him from even considering it as an option. Quentin grudgingly admired the logistical sense of it. There were only forty people on the DimCorp staff, so using the river as a border saved a lot of manpower.

"So yeah, the gate," Quentin said with a chuckle.

"How long has it been since anyone here saw the camp in daylight?" Bob asked.

"No one has been there besides Mazik and his crew since the- the revolt- since we came out," Viho said haltingly. "They only go at night, and never past the outer buildings."

"I was afraid of that," Bob said. "It's safe to assume that a lot has changed in, what, four years? Five?"

"Almost five years," Mazik confirmed. He touched the scar on his cheek. "I was twelve then."

"We need to scout the camp," Bob said. Quentin heard the reluctance in his voice, and looked over at him. "It's a dangerous thing to even consider, but we really need to know what we're walking into."

It didn't seem like a doable thing to Quentin at all. Mazik was the only one crazy enough to swim in the river, and he would have to sneak around in the dark and try to get a sense of the place. The only other way to do it was to walk up to the front gate and ask for a tour. They wouldn't gain much from the effort and stood to lose a lot, if Mazik got caught or attacked in the river by the natural wardens. While it would be helpful to scout out the camp, it was far too risky. They were just going to have to wing it when they got there.

"I will go," Tocho said. "Mazik can guide me to the camp, and I will see what I can see."

"Okay," Bob agreed. "Tocho and I will go. When we come back, we will make a plan for that part of things."

"Whoa, wait a minute," Quentin protested. Had Tocho and Bob completely lost their grip on reality? "We can't have you two walking into the heart of Mordor. What if something happened to you? We'd be in a mess."

"We're not going to walk down the middle of the street, whistling a song. We'll stay outside the camp and have Mazik bring Keme out to the river so we can talk to him. Crocodiles are about the worst thing we have to worry about." Bob grinned at Quentin. "It'll be fine. We'll have a lot more information to work with, and that's totally worth a small risk."

Quentin didn't think the risk was very small at all, but he couldn't bring himself to challenge Bob about it in front of everyone after their earlier argument. He tried to ignore the sudden tightness in his chest, and the hot, greasy queasiness in his stomach that accompanied it.

Later that evening, Quentin and Eissa walked down to the lake. The sun was already behind the mountains, softening the glow of the sky into a hazy gold. Quentin climbed up on a big white rock at the edge of the water, and slowly turned around, taking in the panorama.

"This place is incredible," he said after a moment, as he hopped down. "What's the equivalent location in our dimension? Panama, maybe, or Costa Rica?"

"Yeah, somewhere around there. They're growing stuff year-round here, so we've got to be right on the equator."

It was difficult to stop thinking about the mission and just enjoy the scenery. Bob's decision to scout the DimCorp camp was an unexpected punch in the gut. Worry weighed him down, an anchor that constantly reminded him that nothing was going according to plan, and everything was far more dangerous than he had been prepared for. It was a recurring theme in his life lately. He sat down and leaned back against the rock, facing the lake. Eissa plopped down beside him. The surface of the lake was like glass, flawlessly reflecting the distant volcano and the sky.

She leaned against him, putting her head on his shoulder. "Do you question yourself about what we're doing?"

"Which part?" He meant it to be funny, but neither of them laughed.

She sat up and rubbed her face. "I don't know. Whether we should be pushing the Bribri to do this. Whether Bob and Tocho should be trying to do this stupid recon. Whether we should just pack up and go back to the island." She laughed abruptly, a short, barking chop that echoed flatly off the rocks. "Seriously, though. Do you think about that fact that we could go back home to our dimension and just start over somewhere new? Go someplace that Carl Holt can't find us, like Seattle, and just go back to being normal people?"

Quentin didn't answer right away. He was afraid to be too honest about it. He had second-guessed himself a hundred times just since they arrived in this dimension, but that didn't feel like the right thing to say. It wasn't that he was ashamed, although he was. It was mostly that he didn't want her worrying about him and being distracted by that, which he knew was exactly what she would do.

"Oh, it's crossed my mind," he said. "Now that you know all of this exists though, could you go back to a regular life?"

"Could you?"

As an IT tech, he lived a decent life. While sitting in a cubicle, resetting passwords and solving computer problems for people had paid the bills, it certainly hadn't been fulfilling. On the other hand, it had been much safer than his current lifestyle, and much more predictable. Which did he value more, fulfillment or security?

"I don't know," he said. "I mean, my life was essentially pointless, before. Spending all my time working so that someone else could get rich, while I stayed ten feet on this side of the survival line, sitting around drinking coffee and diagnosing all the problems of society in my free time… what would I be going back to? None of it means anything."

A huge white bird glided across the lake, the tips of its wings nearly touching the surface. They watched it until it was out of sight, lost in the trees on the distant shore. It was funny how much his opinion of his own lifestyle had changed. Three months ago, he'd been pretty smug, secure in his routine. He had his problems, of course, but nothing that his next raise wouldn't solve, or even his sister sticking with a job and paying some bills around the house. The time spent with Eissa, dissecting politics and economics, made him feel like a brilliant thinker, an analyst, solving the world's problems. How small his universe had been.

"I agree that this new perspective has permanently fucked up my ability to think small," Eissa said. "But in terms of stress, and relative safety and comfort, this is keeping us both a little strung out."

Quentin smiled. On the scale of broadening one's horizons, this whole dimension-hopping experience was off the charts. Would he ever be satisfied with staying in one place again? She was right about the stress, though. "I know. I keep telling myself that we're just getting started. Once we've been living this lifestyle for six months or a year, it will feel a lot more comfortable."

"That's true," she agreed. "This kind of thing definitely takes some getting used to."

He smoothed out the wrinkles in his pants. Eissa was handling most of this far better than he ever would have imagined, but he still worried about her. She had spent years in therapy after her last time in a war, and now they were flirting with the same sort of scenario again. PTSD sufferers probably shouldn't be in situations like this. Everything they were about to do was a potential trigger that could push her over the edge, but he had been so wrapped up in his own anxieties about it that he hadn't really talked to her about how she was handling everything.

"Is the stress messing with your PTSD?" he asked quietly. "I mean, you seem fine, but there's been a lot going on."

She drew in a deep breath, and let it out in a long, slow sigh. "Not like I thought it would. I mean, I had that anxiety attack when we went to the Genesis Dimension, but that's the only really stressful thing that's happened so far. I guess we'll know in a few days if it's going to happen again."

Quentin gave a rueful smile. "Yeah, I guess so."

He felt guilty about putting her in a situation that might exacerbate her emotional problems, even though she volunteered to do this before he did. He was glad that she would be readying her triage center when the confrontation took place, and not on the front line.

"Hey, we've got each other, and we've got Bob and Tocho," she reminded him. "Neither one of us is the Lone Ranger here."

"That's right. You might need to remind me of that every ten minutes or so. I keep feeling like I'm in over my head with no lifeguard around."

"You're going to be okay," she reassured him, squeezing his hand. "I've got you."

He hoped she was right. The stress that was constantly boiling in his stomach made it seem impossible to feel confident, but her reassurances at least calmed him down to a state of medium discomfort, which was a major improvement over the state of borderline panic that he kept defaulting to.

They watched together as the sky over the lake turned darker and darker shades of purple, until eventually stars began to appear. The familiar site of Venus grounded him in a way that nothing else had so far, and he was filled with joy for the first time in days as he watched it rise.

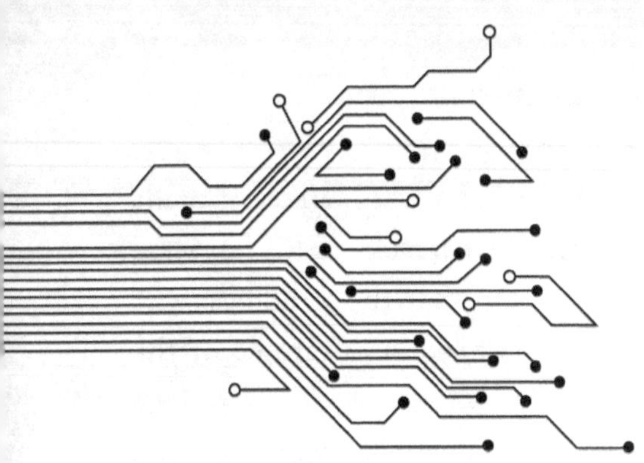

CHAPTER 7

"**B**ader!"

Vincent Macalister grinned as he heard the chair legs crash to the floor out on the porch. Bader never made him shout twice, always did what he was told, and he was ruthless. If he had twenty Bader clones, he could take over the world. He wiped the smile off his face as Bader opened the office door.

"What's up, boss?"

"Find Morgan Gage, and tell him to get his ass in here."

"I'm on it, boss. I just saw him going toward the cane mill."

Macalister thought for a moment and stopped Bader as he was reaching for the door.

"Check that." He climbed to his feet and grabbed his hat and whip off the file cabinet. "I'll walk down there. Who's with him?"

"Nobody's patrolling with him. He's probably spot-checking." Bader backed through the doorway and followed Macalister down the hall.

"Alright," Macalister said, stepping out on to the porch. "You stay here and hold the fort down. I'll be back."

He walked across the square to the far side of the warehouse and turned right toward the mill. The afternoon sun cast a deep shadow on this side of the building, and while it didn't make the humidity any less of a wet blanket, it made the heat a little more bearable. The barracks to his left were bathed in sunshine, and he noticed that the windows were dirty. He made a mental note to make an example of the cleaning crew soon.

When he got to the end of the warehouse, he stopped cold, consumed by fury at the sight before him.

"What in the hell is going on here?" he shouted, striding into the open.

In front of him, Morgan Gage was pushing the long pole of the cane-grinding mill along with a slave. Gage had his back turned as Macalister approached, and Macalister felt a bit of pleasure as Gage jumped, but it didn't dampen his rage any.

"I'm just keeping the mill going while Keme's at the outhouse," Gage said, his face reddening.

This was exactly what was wrong with Gage and his thoughts on leadership. If this was the kind of shit they were teaching at the Academy these days, they might as well close down shop. How were the guards supposed to respect him when he put himself in the slave's position? There were six guards here, all watching their supervisor push the goddamn pole. How did he expect the slaves to respect him? Sure, they probably appreciated that he was willing to work, since that was less they had to do, but being lazy and respecting leadership were two very different things.

Macalister clenched his fists. He really wanted to whip Gage's ass right here in front of everyone, but that wouldn't solve any of his problems. If anything, it would make them worse. He set aside the urge, and focused his attention on the real problem, which was preventing Gage from causing problems with the gold. That's why he had come out here in the first place.

"You're the goddamn second in command of this shit-show," Macalister said. He pointed at one of the slaves filling buckets at the base of the mill. "You, get your ass over there and replace him. Now!"

The boy jumped up, knocking over his bucket as he tried to hurry to Gage.

"You're lucky that bucket was empty," Macalister snarled, narrowing his eyes. "If you'd spilled a bucket of cane juice, I'd have taken it out of your back."

Gage stepped back and let the slave replace him. The boy could barely reach the pole, but he made a show of giving it all he had. Gage pointed him to the end of the pole where it was closer to the ground and walked over to Macalister.

"Are you all right, boss?"

Macalister began walking, and Gage fell in beside him. They moved through the cane processing area, and onto the road that led past the Bribri camp into the cane fields. He wasn't used to screening his words, but it was important that he handle this properly, and he considered and rejected a dozen statements before settling on one.

"Why the fuck do you do shit like that?" Macalister finally asked.

"What, helping out with the work?"

"Yes, helping out with the work," Macalister mimicked him. "You don't see me acting like that, do you?" He realized that he sounded like an asshole, and he needed to tone it down. Putting Gage on the defensive would make this harder than it already was, but Macalister found it almost impossible to let it go.

"It's a leadership technique," Gage said. "When I show the Bribri that I'm not too good to get in there and sweat a little and get my hands dirty, they respect me for it."

"Why do you care if they respect you? They're fucking cavemen. They don't mean shit."

Gage glanced at him. "Maybe you ought to get in there and try it sometime. You'd be surprised how much harder people will work for you when they respect you."

Macalister's eyes turned black, his fist clenching painfully tight around the handle of the whip. He could feel his nails digging into his palms, which helped him regain a bit of control. "You'd better watch your tone, buck." He shook his head and forced himself to calm down. His first instinct was to punch Gage in the mouth for that comment, but he was out here to get him to commit to the plan and punishing him wouldn't get them there. "You've got some crazy ideas about leadership. They sure as hell didn't teach shit like that when I was in the Academy."

He stopped at the edge of the first cane field. The sugarcane towered over their heads, blocking out everything else on the horizon. The dark green leaves rustled in the occasional breeze. Macalister didn't come out here very often. It made him feel like an ant wandering around in the tall grass, insignificant, and that wasn't a feeling that he liked. The momentary discomfort gave him enough of a mental break to change gears, and he finally moved on to the real purpose of the conversation.

"How much sugar do we have in reserve? If we didn't cut another blade of grass out here, how long would we be able to keep making chocolate?"

Gage ticked off his fingers, counting under his breath.

"With what we've got cut, plus what's already processed in the warehouse, I'd say about a month."

Macalister grunted. He knew the answer, of course, but this was about getting Gage to take ownership of the chocolate trade. "We've got six cacao groves in rotation, and four cane fields. We're turning two of the cane fields into groves, which will cut our sugar production in half."

"Right," Gage agreed.

Macalister turned, and began walking the other direction toward the cacao groves. Gage jogged a few steps to catch up. He'd been toying with this idea for a few days, and it seemed like the best way to maximize their gold intake while keeping the corporate bean counters satisfied. If Gage went for this, Macalister's worries about Gage turning him in to Corporate would be over. *If.* He had to be careful with this conversation, diplomatic. Not his usual approach to things, and the rocky start made it even more awkward for him.

"What if we expanded the plantation again?" Macalister asked. "What if we left the cane fields like they are, and added three or four cacao groves to the other end?"

Gage glanced at him. "Do you want my honest opinion?"

"You'd better be honest with me every time you tell me something. I'm relying on you." Macalister tucked the whip into his belt and jammed his hands in his pockets, waiting for Gage to continue.

"Alright. I think that we're at the absolute limit right now. We've got people doing two and three jobs, trying to keep it all running. We just don't have the manpower to get any bigger." Gage looked around, sweeping his arm to take in the expanse of the plantation. "You have to admit, we're doing a pretty impressive job as it is."

They walked in silence for a few minutes. The cane fields to their right gave way to the shorter cacao trees. The wider alleys between the rows afforded glimpses of the river at the far end of the orchard. Macalister was careful to keep the smile off his face, as Gage played right into his hand. The next move was the trickiest. If he pushed it, Gage would bolt, no question. Every word counted.

"What if we… recruited… more help?" Macalister tried to sound halting, but casual, as if he weren't sure of himself or his idea. This was the dangerous bit, the part that could change the game. It was also the hardest part for Macalister to deliver, as making himself sound vulnerable went against every fiber of his being, and was something he had absolutely no experience with. Gage stopped and stared at him, and Macalister turned to face him.

"Are you- are you suggesting that we go capture some more slaves?"

Macalister looked down at his feet for a moment, then out at the cacao grove beside them. "I'm tossing ideas out there, and we're discussing them," he said carefully. "That's all. I just want your opinion."

He could feel Gage's eyes on him, probing, and he was afraid he'd overplayed it. Collecting their own slaves was a serious violation of protocol, of course, and Gage would be naturally opposed to the idea of breaking major company rules. Maybe he should have mentioned the gold again, a little retirement reminder of why they were having this discussion. No, Gage was motivated by principles and ideas more than money. It made him much harder to manipulate. Macalister took a breath, ready to laugh off the idea as a ridiculous joke, when Gage finally spoke.

"We don't have enough guards to do that." Gage shook his head. "Nowhere near enough. I mean, we need twenty-five guys to keep things under control here, which would only give us thirteen to go do that. If somebody got hurt or killed in the process, we'd be in serious trouble."

Macalister nodded thoughtfully, his face calm, while on the inside he was jumping for joy, fist pumping in celebration. The bait had been taken. Now he had to set the hook. Carefully, ever so carefully, as if he had just thought of the idea, he countered Gage's point. "Maybe we could put all the slaves in the warehouse and keep them locked down with three or four guys."

There was a moment of stillness as Gage absorbed the statement. Beyond the plantation wall in the jungle, a monkey screamed shrilly, startling a few birds into flight.

"Yeah, I didn't think about that," Gage admitted. He gave Macalister a sideways glance. "Have you thought about asking DimCorp for more help? I mean, hell, even if we were able to add more workers without losing anyone, we'd have too many to handle with the number of guards that we have now. They've already proved that once."

Anger flashed through him like a bolt of lightning at the reminder of his failure, but he quashed it immediately. They had momentum going in this discussion, and he wasn't about to lose it now. Success was only a hair's breadth away. He needed Gage to trust him and feel like he was taking Gage into his confidence. Gage wasn't stupid, and he would be quick to realize it if Macalister tried to fool him with bullshit. This was a critical response, the logic that would either convince Gage to abandon his commitment to DimCorp's rulebook, or sound the alarm and bring in the DimCorp brass. Macalister was all in, and it was time to show his cards.

"Gage, I know you've got aspirations. Hell, I do too. It's guys like us that make the world go around. So, I'm going to give you some insight on how to make it in this business." He looked around, as if confirming that they had the grove to themselves.

"Here's what they don't teach you in the Academy. There're two kinds of leaders. There's guys like you that walk around with the rulebook, doing exactly what they're told, and then there's cowboys like me that find ways to innovate and get the most out of a situation. You follow me?"

"Yes, boss."

"The Academy is a goddamn factory for rulebook guys. They need lots of them, because that's who runs the show down on the lower levels. So, if that's the kind of career aspirations you've got, then that's fine. But if you want to climb the ladder, you've got to learn how to be a cowboy."

Gage nodded. "I see what you're saying, boss, but I didn't think you wanted me to be a cowboy. You're pretty critical of how I do things, as it is."

Macalister knew he was edging out on thin ice, here. He'd been berating Gage for years about the way he did things, and it was a topic that got them both fired up. Right now, he needed to be calm and not attack, no matter how bad he wanted to pick Gage up and shake him and tell him all the things he was doing wrong. He pictured the golden goblet, the one thing that could bring him down when he needed it, and focused on the feeling it brought him.

"Under my command, I want you to be a rulebook guy, yes. But in the grand scheme of things, I want you to be on the cowboy team. Rulebook guys consult the book to know what to do. Cowboys make decisions. You see the difference?"

Gage's eyes lifted, and Macalister knew he had gotten through. He kept the smile off his face, and let Gage commit himself to Team Macalister.

"I think I do," Gage said. "We need to show the brass that we can exceed expectations without asking them for help; show them how independent and resourceful we are."

"Exactly," Macalister said, clapping him on the shoulder with a grin. "If you can take the project and the resources they assign you and double its output on your own, you show them you can handle bigger projects, more responsibility. That's how you get noticed. We just have to figure out the smartest way to handle the situation."

He watched Gage out of the corner of his eye as he pretended to look out across the cacao grove. Gage looked down. He was clearly thinking hard, and Macalister stood in silence, waiting. The worst of it was over, and somehow, he had pulled it off. He should have realized sooner that Gage would respond to career advancement more than retirement money. He was young, and retirement was too far away to be important. Either way, they had gotten there.

It felt like a massive weight had been lifted from his shoulders. Now that Gage was on board, the gold was safe, and there would be more coming. He had time to breathe, and prepare for his exit, rather than rushing through it, trying to dodge a swinging axe.

"So, I think the best bet would be to try to recapture the rest of the Bribri, huh?" Gage swatted a fly away from his face as he looked up. "I mean, they already know the work, and they speak the language."

"That's the upside," Macalister said. "The downside is that they got away with revolting once already. That might make them harder to force back into the system." The breeze kicked up for a moment, whispering through the leaves and cooling the sweat on his neck.

"We might be able to get them to come back voluntarily," Gage said. "If we give them the choice to avoid an armed invasion, they just might take it. I mean, we do have half their tribe as bargaining power."

Macalister was rocked by the suggestion. His first impulse was to scoff at it, but he had to admit that it was worth looking at. They could undoubtedly break Viho by threatening to torture the slaves that were on the inside of the plantation. Viho was an old pussy, vulnerable because of his emotional attachment to everyone, and taking him a box with some child's amputated ears in it would probably be enough for him to line up the whole village and march them through the front gate. A box of hands would be even more effective, but it would make the kid useless as a worker. The more he thought about it, the more he liked the idea.

Macalister took a few steps down the road, forcing Gage to follow. "You might just have something there, Gage, you just might."

Gage smiled faintly, his hands clasped behind his back. "Is that the cowboy thinking you were looking for?"

Macalister laughed, surprised by the question. "It's a good start." He turned to face Gage. "I need you to be on board with me. I can't do this without you. Are you with me?"

Gage looked him in the eye earnestly. "I'm with you, boss."

Macalister clapped him on the shoulder again. "Let's go eat some supper. We'll sit down and figure out a plan in a few days, once the trade run gets back."

Macalister felt good about the conversation. Putting Gage in charge of the slave-gathering project would give him a sense of ownership. Once he had spearheaded a slave capture, he would be invested in it, and there would be no turning back.

His spirits lifted as they walked back to camp, and he felt better than he had in weeks. DimCorp might think they were running this show again, but there was only one sheriff in this town, and his name was Vincent Motherfucking Macalister.

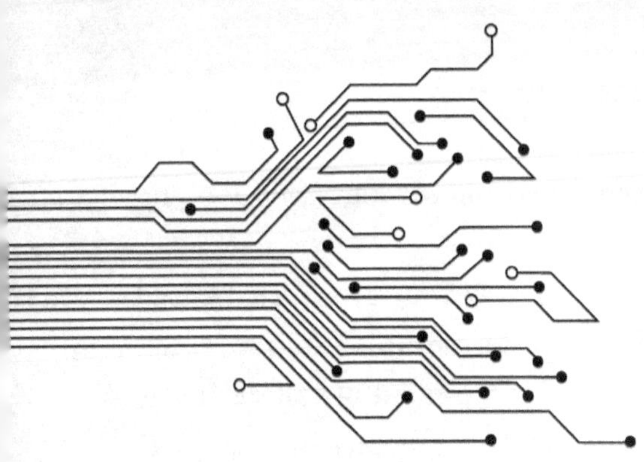

CHAPTER 8

Morgan Gage played the bizarre conversation over in his mind as they returned to camp. Macalister was clearly trying to coerce him, and it involved violating DimCorp rules in a big way. All the fatherly mentoring talk was so out of character that Macalister might as well have been holding a sign that said *I'm trying to screw you over.* Capturing slaves without corporate authorization was a huge no-no. There was no way to hide a doubled workforce from the corporate auditors. Even if this whole crazy scheme worked, it was a very short-term thing. They would get caught at some point, and it would end his career. Why would Macalister even consider it?

The most obvious thing that came to mind was that Macalister wasn't playing a long-term game. He had to know he couldn't get away with it for more than a year or two. That meant he was planning to get out before it blew up in his face. And since he hadn't mentioned anything about leaving, he was probably hoping to leave Gage standing there holding the bag. Interesting. Was this about the gold, or was there something more that he was missing? He needed time to think it out.

"I'm going to stop off at the outhouse, boss. I'll catch up with you later." Gage tried to act nonchalant and gave Macalister a little wave as he turned off the road at the edge of camp.

"Alright." Macalister walked on without even looking at him.

Everything was happening way too fast. Sure, he had been horrified at the way Macalister ran this camp from the day he got here, but as the new kid fresh out of college, it was hard to know whether it was just the difference between academia and the real world, or if Macalister was actually doing things that DimCorp wouldn't approve of. He had learned a lot in his few years here, though, and he was confident that Macalister was wrong, but with the DimGate being out of service, he couldn't talk to anyone about it. That was tough, and out of desperation in the last year, he had begun talking about it to Keme. He might be a slave, but Keme was still a strong leader, and he understood the dynamics of good communication. Still, there was a big difference between acknowledging a leadership problem, and going over your boss's head to Corporate and accusing him of gross misconduct.

Up until this point, he really hadn't even committed himself to reporting Macalister. He fantasized about it, and it had definitely been a mistake to share that dream with Keme, but now he found himself in the awkward position of either going through with it immediately, or violating his own code of ethics and the company code of conduct. All this in a matter a day.

He stood beside the outhouse until Macalister was out of sight, and then made his way to his quarters. He needed to formulate a plan, and he didn't want any distractions while he was thinking. The weight of his future was crushing him, making him painfully aware of what was in the balance.

He slipped in the door of the barracks and walked to the far end. He had a private room away from the main floor, and while it didn't afford him a lot of privacy, something was better than nothing. He closed the door and stretched out on his bunk, making sure that his boots were hanging off the end.

What would it mean if he went along with Macalister? Could he justify that to himself? After all, he would be following the orders of his superior officer. Would DimCorp buy that if they found out what was going on, or would he end up in jail along with Macalister? Assuming Macalister didn't manage to execute his escape strategy, of course. There was still that angle to consider.

The idea of going to jail jolted him. Was that really a possibility? Gathering slaves was considered a high-risk operation, and DimCorp had specially-trained teams that did that. They also left a security detail in place for a few months after such an operation to protect the camp from a retaliation strike. If they tried to gather more slaves on their own and something went wrong, they would be buried under the company jail. Well, assuming they were still alive. Shit.

What was the worst-case scenario? If they did have to resort to violence to get the rest of the Bribri back in the plantation, and that was a reasonable assumption, then it was fair to assume that they would lose a few guards in the process. Say five, as a conservative estimate. If he woke up one day a year from now, and Macalister and his room full of gold were gone, he would have to explain everything to DimCorp when they showed up. How they had turned five hundred slaves into a thousand, why guards had died without being reported to headquarters, where Macalister had gone, why he hadn't said anything to Corporate about it at any point. The very thought made him want to throw up.

If he were to try to turn Macalister in, how would that go? DimCorp was just as susceptible to politics as anyplace else. He really didn't know Macalister's supervisor, Ocklin, or what their relationship was like. Ocklin hadn't shown up here since the Gate came back on, so there was that. Still, it was risky. If Ocklin sided with Macalister, which he might, considering he hadn't actually done anything yet other than stockpile some gold and try to run his chocolate business on the sly, then Gage could kiss his career goodbye.

On the other hand, if Ocklin did see that Macalister had gone rogue, it would make sense for him to remove Macalister, and maybe even put Gage in charge. That would give him the power to make things better, and run the camp the way it should be run. In that scenario, Bader would be a problem. Bader would be liable to kill him in his sleep for turning Macalister in. He would have to be dealt with right away.

There were just too many unknowns, and not enough time to figure them out. The first problem of turning Macalister in would be the physical logistics of it. Macalister's computer kept track of every user ID that was used to activate the DimGate. If he checked the log and saw that Gage had crossed to the Genesis Dimension without permission, how would he explain that?

Permission: that was the key. He needed a plausible excuse to go over there with Macalister's knowledge. Could he put in for vacation? No, not with all the stuff that he was supposed to be getting done, that wouldn't get approved. What if he feigned an illness and had to go to the medical treatment center? That might work. He sat up, swinging his feet off the side of the bed.

Once he got to DimCorp headquarters, he could go to the human resources department and talk to someone about the situation. That would be safer than going straight to Ocklin. Yes, that's exactly what he would do.

He stretched his arms overhead with a smile. The weight of indecision was lifted from his shoulders, and he felt good about his plan. Now it would just be a matter of timing and putting it into action. He had until the next trade convoy to get sick enough to warrant a trip to the MTC. He'd better start putting on a show now. He stood up and headed for the mess hall.

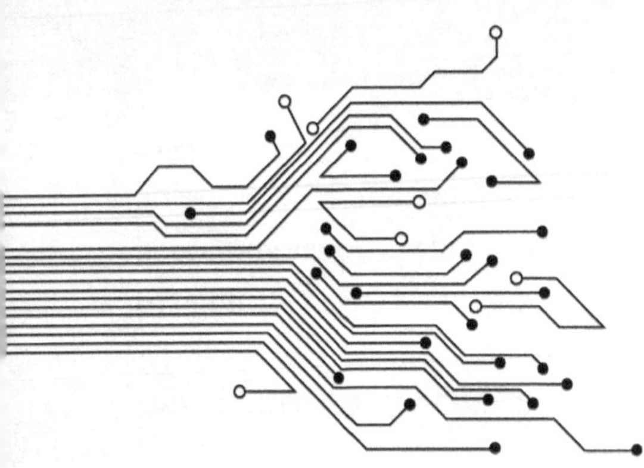

CHAPTER 9

Quentin and Eissa sat on the front porch of Viho's house, along with Viho and Tahki Ana. They were eating baked fish and roasted vegetables, which they had helped harvest from the community garden earlier that afternoon.

"This is amazing," Eissa said around a mouthful of potatoes. "If I had paid $20 for this, I'd feel like I was robbing you."

Tahki Ana smiled with a questioning look on her face. "I don't understand what you mean."

"Money isn't really a thing around here," Quentin said. "The reference doesn't work in a moneyless society."

He swallowed some water and tried to come up with a simple explanation of money. It was harder than he expected. Discussing the economy with Eissa proved to be challenging at times, and she knew all about money. Getting it down to a few sentences for someone who had no basis for comparison? It was far too complicated. While he was thinking, his attention was drawn to a figure running up the street on the far side of the square.

"I think that's Mazik," Viho said. "Why would he be back so soon, I wonder? And where are Bob and Tocho? He should not have left them out there alone."

The runner stumbled as he entered the square, falling to the ground in a heap. He pushed himself up slowly, and every movement displayed a combination of exhaustion and determination. Quentin set his plate down and stood up, watching. A bad feeling crept into his gut, killing his appetite.

"It *is* Mazik," Tahki Ana said, rising to stand beside him. "Something's wrong."

The four of them ran across the yard, and Viho caught Mazik as he stumbled again. He bent down and lifted Mazik onto his shoulder, and carried him back to the porch.

"Hold the curtain back," he commanded. Eissa ran ahead and grabbed the curtain, and held it out of the way as he climbed the steps. Quentin put a hand on his back to support him, and they made their way inside. Viho carefully lowered Mazik to the floor.

"Are you hurt?" he asked, pushing the hair away from Mazik's eyes. "Tell me what's wrong. Why have you come back alone? Where are Tocho and Bob?"

Mazik opened his eyes. His chest heaved, and his body was coated with sweat and grime.

"I'm not hurt," he gasped. "Just- just give me- a minute. I gotta- catch my breath."

He lay back on the floor, sucking in great gusts of air and blowing it out. He waved his hand, gesturing for a drink. Tahki caught Eissa's eye and pointed to the bucket.

"I've got the water," Eissa said, turning to the door. "Elevate his head a bit with a pillow or something."

Viho grabbed one of the small pillows near the wall and jammed it under Mazik's head. After a drink and a minute to breathe, Mazik looked considerably better. He sat up and leaned wearily against the wall.

"Tocho and Bob- got caught by DimCorp," he said. "I

ran. All the way back here. Many miles." He drank some more water, as the news sank into the group.

"Oh, shit," Quentin cried in dismay. The information was a lightning bolt, instantly frying his senses. "Oh, no, what- how did that happen? What happened?" He staggered back against the far wall and slid down to a seated position. The others were similarly shocked, and the room was filled with the confused babble of repeated questions and exclamations.

Mazik took another drink before answering, and waved his hand for silence. An expectant hush fell over them. At last, he told them what happened.

"When we got to the DimCorp camp, they wanted to see everything while it was daytime." Mazik wiped his mouth with his hand. His breathing was starting to slow down, which made it easier to understand him. "We crawled through the woods to the edge so they could see the front gate. Then we moved to a different place. Bob drew pictures of the camp. Then we got to the river."

"Don't tell me they wanted to swim with the crocodiles," Eissa said.

Quentin wanted to tell her to shut up, to stop inter-rupting, but his brain remained disconnected from his body. All he could do was sit and listen and try to comprehend it all. It was an odd sensation, as part of his mind was frozen, a helpless victim along for the ride, while the other part was working overtime, processing thoughts and ramifications at a furious rate.

"Bob wanted to swim around the wall and sneak in the cacao grove. He said he couldn't see enough with the wall in the way."

"Oh, Bob," Tahki murmured.

Quentin shook his head, finally able to speak again. "I should have made a bigger deal about them going. I can already guess what happened."

Mazik glanced up at him. "Bob didn't listen to me. I said we should wait until dark. He just climbed down the bank and started sneaking down towards the wall. Tocho said I could come back here, but I didn't want them to get in trouble, so I went, too."

"Were there crocodiles everywhere?" Eissa asked.

"Jesus, Eissa, let him tell us what happened," Quentin snapped.

"Sorry, bite my damn head off." Her face turned scarlet at the public rebuke.

He felt bad for being mean to her, but this was serious. Like, end of the world serious. Bob and Tocho were the center of everything, the knowledge base, the experience, the plans, everything. They were the pilots of this whole expedition. If they were captured, that meant there was no one to fly the plane.

"I didn't see any crocs," Mazik said. "But who knows? They sit on the bottom of the river, and it's muddy. Anyway, we walked down to the wall under the trees, and then we had to swim out to go around the wall. It goes out into the river a ways."

Quentin nodded, trying to picture it.

"That grove was empty, so we went up to the front. I saw people working in the grove across the road. Bob wanted to talk to Keme, so I ran across the road to see if he was there. I found out he was working the cane mill, so I slipped back across. I told them we can't go see Keme, he is in the camp. Bob said he was going to go see Keme anyway."

"Bob is a stubborn man," Viho said, patting Mazik's arm. "I know you tried to keep him safe."

Mazik shook his head. "I led them around the long way. We stayed in the cacao groves and the cane fields all the way up to the edge of camp. We almost got caught twice by guards. Then I had to sneak into the camp and get Keme. There were guards all over the place. That was the worst part."

"I know it was," Viho said. "You have the heart of a lion. Did you find Keme?"

"Yes, he was at the mill. I stayed across the street, and caught his attention. He came over, but he was very angry. He asked me why I was there in the daytime, trying to get everyone in trouble. I told him Bob and Tocho were in the cane, and wanted to talk to him. He said he only had two minutes, that the guard thought he was at the outhouse."

He paused for another drink. His breathing had slowed to normal, and Tahki wiped the sweat from his face with her sleeve.

"Keme ran into the cane field with me. Bob told him what we were trying to do. Keme said Morgan Gage might agree to it, but Macalister would never say yes. He also said there is a trade convoy headed north in two days. He drew some pictures for Bob, then he ran back to the mill.

"I thought we were going to go back to the river, but Bob wanted to sneak around and look at the rest of the camp, like we did in the forest out front. We crossed a road, and that's when they got caught. I was already in the tall cane on the other side, and someone shouted to get on the ground or they would get shot. I moved in a few rows so they couldn't see me, and then ran down to where I could see them through a break. The guards had Bob and Tocho face down on the ground, and were searching them. I slipped away as quiet as I could, and came back here."

The room fell quiet. Quentin's mind was numb, as if his head was floating on a string above his body. He would have fallen if he wasn't already sitting. He tried to think of something to say, something appropriate as the de facto leader of the group.

Obviously, they would have to find a way to rescue Bob and Tocho. It was going to be difficult. Everyone would have to pitch in. He was working on how he would address them, when he realized that someone was slapping him repeatedly.

"What- hey," he muttered, raising his arms in protest.

"Can you hear me?" Eissa asked. She pried his eyelid open and looked closely at him. Her eyes were red, and he knew that she was trying not to cry.

"Yeah, yeah," Quentin said, pulling his head away. "Did you just slap me?"

"You started to pass out," she said. "Don't you go into shock on me. How many fingers am I holding up?"

"I'm okay." He sat up straight. "Four fingers, now give me a second so I can think."

Tahki brought him some water. He gave her a smile of thanks and accepted the cup. He felt a bit dizzy, but the cool water helped re-center his brain.

"This is bad," Viho said. "This is very bad. We should not have agreed to this."

"How do we get them out?" Quentin asked. "Can we sneak in at night and get them?"

The others looked at him in silence.

"We can't just abandon them. We've got to do something." Eissa's voice broke, and she buried her face in her hands.

Quentin climbed to his feet. His knees were weak, and he steeled himself against the desire to collapse in a heap. With courage that he didn't feel at all, he tried to take charge of the situation.

"Look, we have to reason this out," he said. "I'm not saying we go charge the front gate, okay? Let's figure out what our options are for rescuing them. We've got to be logical. If we let our emotions drive us, then we'll just end up in a bigger mess."

He scrubbed his face with his hands and took a deep breath. "Okay, so I guess our options are either a front gate rescue, or a river rescue. I guess we can choose between day and night, too."

"You always have crap options," Eissa said. "You aren't very good at this."

"Well, we seem to find ourselves in crap situations." He was grateful that she was trying to lighten things up a bit, but he couldn't quite bring himself to chuckle. His heart was too heavy for that.

"We can't rescue them," Viho said. "We must stop this now, before anyone else gets hurt. No rescue, and no mission."

Quentin stared at Viho, slack-jawed with incomprehension. He opened his mouth to argue, but no words came out. Why would Viho say that? He must have misunderstood. They couldn't *not* rescue them, that wasn't even conceivable.

"I will help you rescue them." Mazik climbed to his feet and glared at Viho. "My team is strong. We will sneak into the camp tonight and find them. We will kill the guards and bring Bob and Tocho back."

"You will not," Viho thundered. He rose to his feet like a mountain. "I forbid this."

"You forbid everything," Mazik shouted back. "I am tired of letting them do what they want to us. I see Keme, with scars all over him. Don't you want to stop them from beating him for you? He is your brother. He is probably being beaten right now, as we speak. Don't you care?"

Viho raised his arm to strike Mazik, but Tahki grabbed his fist.

"DimCorp will not make us fight one another," she said softly. "I forbid this."

The flash of anger between them hit Quentin like a slap to the face, clearing the cobwebs from his mind. Tahki Ana's voice was filled with quiet authority as she took control of the situation.

Tahki Ana released Viho's fist and turned to Mazik. "I know your rage, grandson. I feel it, too. If you are to be a wise warrior though, you must learn to think with your head, and fight with your heart. If you think with your heart, you will get killed. Let us talk on this with our heads. When we decide on our action, that's when you use your rage."

"Yes, grandmother," Mazik whispered. He looked away from her, back to Quentin.

"She's right," Quentin said. He tried to keep his voice neutral, and not show the sense of loss and failure that was sweeping over him. Now that he was over the initial shock, his mind was racing. "We have to think this out. If we just attack the camp, then the long-term plan goes out the window. We'll be in that situation that we talked about yesterday, with four hundred more guards showing up, or four thousand. We might save Bob and Tocho, but the Bribri would lose in the long run."

Viho nodded.

"But we can't just leave them there," Quentin said. "They're our lifeline in this whole multi-dimension thing. I wouldn't know how to function without them. We've got to figure something out."

"What does that leave?" Eissa asked.

"Fuck if I know."

Tahki spoke up, and their eyes turned to her. "We must let this rest. We have only just learned of it. We cannot find the answer so quickly. Go, wash your face with the sunshine and let the wind still your heart. We will talk on this tonight."

Quentin marveled at her wisdom, and felt like a complete fraud for trying to take charge of the situation. He should have realized that they were all responding emotionally, even after he convinced himself that he was being logical. He let out a shaky sigh.

"Good plan," he said. "I could use some fresh air."

"You want to walk down to the lake?" Eissa asked.

"Yeah, let's do that. A good walk will help me calm down and sort this out."

By the time they made it to the water, the feeling of dread in his chest had shrunk down to a manageable level. His heart was finally beating normally again, which was a relief. He worried that he was wearing it out with all the stress he had put on it recently.

They were in a hell of a fix. If they approached the camp in force to make a hostile rescue, DimCorp would know the Bribri was involved, and that was bad. That also ran a high risk of injuries and death. If they snuck in at night, they would have to figure out where Bob and Tocho were being held, which would be almost impossible in the dark, not to mention the danger of going in the river. That danger would multiply when going back out if anyone was injured or bleeding, as that would draw the caribes and the crocodiles.

"What the fuck are we going to do?" Eissa asked. "I tried to hold it together in there, but I'm freaking the fuck out."

He glanced at her. She was crying, which he expected, but the rage and terror that fought for control of her expression sent a bolt of fear through him.

"Hey, hey. I need you to be in control, here. We have to handle this, and that means I need you."

"I'm trying, but this is some serious shit. How are we going to fix this? It's not like I can march in there and tell Macalister to let them go." She scrubbed her face with her sleeve. "This is totally fucked."

Her anger was taking over, and Quentin relaxed a little. A panic attack was the last thing they needed, but as long as she was more pissed off than scared, she was okay.

"It's a lot to process," he said. "Right now, I just want to go in there with machine guns blazing and wipe them out."

"Well, now you know how I felt when you got arrested in DimCorp headquarters and hauled off," Eissa said. "That took ten years off my life."

"I get it," he said. "I thought I understood before, but this is certainly a perspective-changer. Now I really feel terrible about that. This is a hell of a thing to put someone through."

Eissa shot him a grateful smile, but then her face darkened. "You know, we haven't said it out loud, but it's possible that they're already dead."

Quentin picked up a rock and tried to skip it across the lake. It bounced twice and sank. It was possible that they were dead, yes, but he really couldn't consider it. If anything, this experience was showing him how much he needed them, how ill-prepared he was to do anything on his own. For that reason alone, they had to get them back, not to mention the myriad of other, less-selfish reasons.

"I don't think so," he said after a moment. He wasn't sure if his logic was sound, but it made him feel better to act brave. "They're both pretty wily old guys. I'm sure they're using the auditor routine or something. Macalister can't kill them if he thinks it's even a remote possibility that they work for DimCorp."

"Yeah, that's a good point."

Quentin climbed up on top of the big rock. "I need some time to think. Right now, my brain is going a million miles an hour, and I'm not getting anywhere. I'm going to try to meditate for a few minutes and see if I can slow my thinking down some."

"Okay," she said. "I'm going to walk around a bit."

The late afternoon sun was warm on his back as he sat, but he couldn't enjoy it for more than a second or two at a time. He did the breathing like Tocho had taught him, *focus on the air going in, focus on the air going out,* but his mind refused to cooperate. There was just too much stress. Next, he tried imagery, and imagined a candle burning in the darkness. The idea was to focus only on the candle and not think about anything else, but pushing his thoughts aside turned out to be a physical impossibility, and after a few minutes he gave up. His mind was determined to keep chewing over all the angles and examining possibilities, and it seemed like the least stressful thing to do was to just go with it.

What resources did they have? Aside from the Bribri tribe, they had the supplies they'd brought with them, mostly food and medical supplies. They had the DimGate, which meant they could go get something else, assuming they knew where to go to get it. The DimGate! Could they use it to rescue Bob and Tocho? He would need the exact coordinates that they wanted to be in the DimCorp camp, which he didn't have. This dimension wasn't mapped in the DimGate computer, so there was no way to ensure they were going to the right spot. Even if they managed to get the DimGate inside the plantation, which was a huge assumption, opening the door in the wrong place, such as in front of the guard's barracks, could be disastrous. The moment of elation collapsed into a sigh of depression.

If they were a Special Forces unit or a SWAT team, this would be a totally manageable situation. The reality made it much more intimidating: he was an IT geek, a keyboard cowboy. Eissa was an out-of-work home healthcare nurse with a suitcase full of PTSD issues from her time in the military as a medic. The Bribri? They were undoubtedly good at hunting game, but ultimately, they were a traumatized tribe of indigenous people, half of whom were enslaved. They weren't warriors, they were farmers. Even Mazik, for all his spirit, was just a teenager in desperate need of counseling that he would never get.

Bob and Tocho were incredibly important to him, and he recognized his bias, and tried to set it aside for a moment. From a purely statistical perspective, they were two men, relative strangers to the tribe, both elderly. Was it reasonable to ask a group of younger men to sacrifice their lives so that these two old men might live a few more years? No way.

That meant if a rescue was going to happen, it would have to be done by Eissa and himself. Was that even possible? It didn't seem like it on the surface, especially if it came down to fighting guards. Quentin really wasn't the fighting type, and he was probably incapable of killing someone.

What if no one had to die? He let his attention wander away from the idea of a hostile rescue mission. There had to be another way, some way that wouldn't mess things up for the Bribri, but would get Bob and Tocho out of there safely. How would Bob handle it, if the situation was reversed? If he were able to talk to Bob on the phone right now, what would Bob say?

"Complete the mission."

The sound of his voice startled him. He hadn't intended to say it out loud, but now that he had, he could see the logic in it. He said it again, his voice stronger this time.

"Complete the mission."

The whole concept of the mission was designed to minimize casualties, and maybe prevent them altogether. What if they went ahead with the mission as if nothing had happened? If it was successful, then they would be in leveraged control of the camp soon, anyway, at which point Bob and Tocho could be rescued as part of the deal.

"I got it," he shouted, leaping to his feet. "I got it figured out."

He looked around for Eissa. He finally spotted her, far down the shore. He scrambled down to the ground, and took off running.

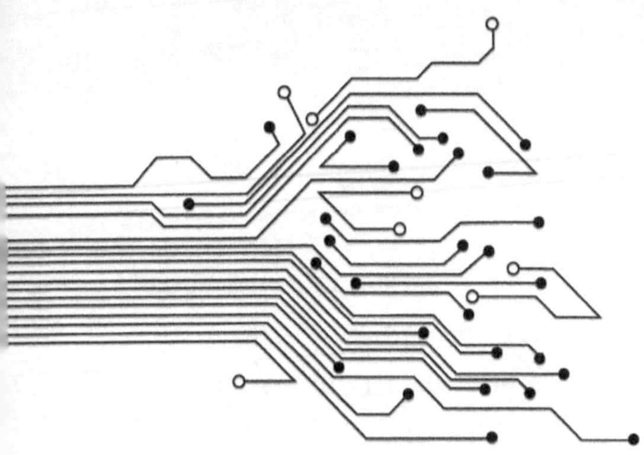

CHAPTER 10

Vincent Macalister sat behind his desk, a piece of paper covered in notes before him. With the tentative commitment from Gage, he had some time to plot his future, rather than his immediate escape. The biggest challenge he had now was time. It took three years for a cacao grove to start producing, and they would have to clear some jungle to make space for it. That would be another year. Four years was probably too long for DimCorp not to realize what he was doing. Really, he would like to be gone by then, but just in case he wasn't, it would be smart to have the extra capacity. Chance favors a prepared mind.

At a minimum, it would take him a year to get out of here, assuming he went through the proper channels and officially retired, but he would be better off to sit tight and build up his gold reserve for five or six more years. He flipped the paper over and made a list of things he needed to figure out.

1. *Cacao for DimCorp*

2. *Cacao and sugar for chocolate trade*

3. *Storing/hiding gold*

4. *Exit strategy*

He flipped the page back over and examined his equations. If his math was right, then his retirement portfolio and savings account had enough money to last him about ten years, assuming he retired in the Genesis Dimension, lived in one of the retirement pods, and didn't try to do anything extravagant. He could only guess at the weight of the gold he had so far, and he didn't know the price of gold anyway, but regardless, he needed more. That meant he had three options. He moved down the page and made another list:

a. *Stop chocolate trade system until new groves produce; send all cacao to DimCorp*

a. *Send limited cacao to DimCorp, continue limited chocolate trade*

a. *Continue full chocolate trade, send nothing to Dim-Corp*

The last option greatly appealed to him, and even made him smile when he thought about it, but he couldn't come up with a way to pull it off. He drew a line through that option, and considered the other two.

DimCorp would want all the cacao, there was no questioning that. If he had been in this situation ten years ago, he probably wouldn't have even thought about not giving them everything. Now, though, he was certain that he wasn't moving up the corporate ladder anymore. The guys his age who were moving up the ladder were several levels ahead of him, and he'd been growing more and more suspicious about the silence he was hearing about his own promotion track before the Gate shut down.

The gold for chocolate deal was an unexpected windfall, and it changed the game. Granted, the food that they got in trade was also important, as were the clothes and tools, but they weren't game changers anymore, now that DimCorp was supplying that stuff again. Now he was in a position to decide his own future, one with much nicer things in it than the mediocre DimCorp retirement package had to offer.

The idea of reducing his gold income in order to give DimCorp more cacao made him feel like they were turning the screws on him even more. He was done being the company man, but he wasn't ready to make his move, so he had to find a delicate balance to keep the game going for a little bit longer. A couple of years at least, and preferably about five more years. The more gold he could stockpile, the better, and the fifth year would be a much bigger gold yield, with the new cacao groves finally producing.

He would have to be careful not to get greedy once that happened. The longer he stayed, the more dangerous it would become, and he couldn't let himself risk losing everything while trying to gain a bit more. Once he got a system in place for melting the gold down and casting it in bars, he could set a hard number on how many bars he needed. A smile softened his face as he imagined a secret door at the back of his closet, one that hid rows and rows of gold bars stacked neatly on the shelves…

Bader burst in the door without knocking, sending Macalister's heart into overdrive. Bader's eyes were wide, and he was breathing hard. Macalister jumped up from his desk, angry that Bader had startled him.

"Goddammit, Paul, what are you doing busting in here like that?" He took in Bader's disheveled appearance, which was highly unusual. Something was obviously wrong.

"Sorry, boss," Bader said, trying to breathe and talk at the same time. "The roving patrol just found two guys out in Field 2, outsiders. I wanted to tell you fast. They took them to the equipment locker for the cane fields, and locked them in there."

"What two guys?" Macalister asked, confusion replacing the anger in his voice. "Slaves trying to escape?"

"No, outside guys. One's an old white guy, the other one's an old local."

"A white guy? Is he DimCorp?" Macalister stepped back from the desk, grabbed his hat and whip, and headed for the door. "Let's go, walk and talk."

"I don't know, boss," Bader said as he closed the door behind them. "I haven't talked to them, just got the word and ran up here to get you."

Macalister walked quickly, his mind racing. If they were DimCorp, they must have come through the DimGate. He wasn't aware of any white people in this dimension, at least not on this continent. That meant the white guy was either Dim-Corp, or a fucking long way from home. If he was DimCorp brass, and the idiot guards had locked him in a cabinet, this could get ugly, and fast.

"I want to know who's on the front gate, and if these guys came through there," Macalister barked. "If they came through the front gate and nobody told me they were here, I'm going to fuck somebody up. If they came through the DimGate, I want to know why nobody saw them until they got all the way to the goddamn fields. If they're DimCorp, I want to know why the fuck they locked them up, instead of bringing them to me."

"I'm on it, boss."

Macalister stormed through the cane processing area, ignoring the guards and slaves as they backed out of his path. He reached the rear of the processing building and turned the corner. The equipment locker was a small shed built on to the back of the building as a place to store shovels, rakes, and other tools used to work the fields. He noted that the tools were all stacked in a heap beside the locker, and a small knot of guards were in front of the door.

"Eyes up," Bader shouted. "Get out of the Boss's way."

The guards separated, allowing Macalister an aisle to the door. He stopped short, and looked around the group.

"Who found them?"

Three guards raised their hands, and the others stepped back further.

"Where?"

"Field 2, boss. They were crossing the center road, headed south."

"Did you identify them?"

"They said they were Internal Affairs."

"Did they have ID?"

"Nothing on them at all, boss. No badge, no nothing."

"If they're IA, why'd you lock them up?" The guard was sweating, and Macalister noted with satisfaction that his lip was quivering as he spoke. "Answers, son, let's go. Why weren't they brought straight to my office?"

"They were soaking wet and muddy, boss. They had to have crossed the river, and we found a few spots where they were laying on the edge of the grove, spying on the camp. That don't seem like IA to me, boss."

Macalister agreed, but decided not to say so. This was a weird situation, and he didn't have a good feeling about it at all. He glared at the guard for a moment longer.

"Open the door."

Another guard jumped over to the door and unlocked the padlock. He pulled the chain out and stepped back as Macalister and Bader approached.

Macalister stopped just outside the door and turned to Bader. He leaned over close, and spoke softly into Bader's ear.

"You do exactly what I tell you to do, when I tell you to do it."

Bader nodded. "Yes, boss."

Macalister turned and stepped in the door.

The two men sat on a long box along the left side of the room. The light coming in through the door put their faces in sharp relief, the far side being almost invisible in the gloom. They were both caked in mud and had clearly been in the river. River water had a muddy yellow tint to it, and these guys were tinted yellow from their hair to their feet.

He stared at them in silence for nearly a full minute. This was usually enough to make people start talking, blabbing on about whatever they thought he wanted to hear. These guys were older, and didn't crack as easily. He shifted tactics.

"So, I hear you're Internal Affairs types, sneaking around and spying on my operation."

The two muddy men glanced at one another. "You must be Vincent Macalister," the one with the beard said. "Nice place you've got here."

Macalister was surprised by that, but he was careful to keep from showing it. He waited.

"I'm Bob Taylor, DimCorp Internal Affairs Special Li-aison." He gestured to the old man seated beside him. "This is Tocho, my assistant and interpreter."

"Special Liaison, huh? How come you don't have ID?"

"We travel innominate, no badge, no gun."

Something didn't feel right, but he wasn't sure enough to call bullshit yet. He decided to let them hang themselves.

"Who's your supervisor and department head?"

"The new department head is Geraldine Stanton, but she's only been there about two years." Bob looked over at Tocho. "Is it two years, or three? When did Dale retire?"

"Closer to three years," Tocho said. "And not a moment too soon."

Bob looked back at Macalister. "Based on your record, you probably know a lot of IA folks. Do you know Geral-dine?"

Macalister ignored the question. "Everyone who's ever been here came through the DimGate and met me in my office. This bullshit about swimming the river and watching my camp tells me you're lying. You don't work for DimCorp. The jungle monkey definitely doesn't work for DimCorp."

"Our DimGate put us on the wrong side of the river," Bob said. "Since we're here to see what your status is, we thought we'd just come over and look around instead of trying to figure out coordinates for an hour."

Macalister nodded at Bader. "Hit him."

Bader stepped forward and slammed his fist into Bob's cheek. His head bounced off the wall with a sickening thud, and blood from his nose splattered across Tocho's arm. He fell forward, but Bader caught him under the arms and sat him back up. His chin dropped down to his chest, so Bader grabbed his hair and lifted his head back up so that Macalister could look him in the eye.

"Now I know you're a fucking liar." Macalister grinned. He was almost giddy with relief to know that they weren't IA, since they would never have their own DimGate. Now he could have some fun.

He leaned in and made sure that Bob was still conscious. "Now, then. I think we understand each other a little better, so let's start over, what do you say? Fresh start?"

Bob moaned, and raised a shaky hand to his face. His nose was trickling blood, and his eyes were glassy. He touched his nose gingerly, then his cheek, before letting his hand fall back to his lap. His eyes rolled up to meet Macalister's.

"I wish you hadn't done that," he said slowly.

"Well, if you don't lie to me again, it won't have to happen again."

He nodded at Bader. Bader released Bob's hair and stepped back over beside Macalister.

"Okay, fresh start." Macalister clapped his hands and smiled. "Who are you, and what were you doing spying on my camp?"

Bob looked at Tocho, then back at Macalister.

"I think we had a misunderstanding," he said slowly. "Do you know what 'Internal Affairs Special Liaison' means? We don't generally get the red-carpet treatment when we show up, but this is starting off pretty badly."

Macalister nodded at Bader again. This time Bader punched him in the stomach, driving all the air out of his lungs. Bob crashed to the floor, landing hard on his shoulder and gasping for breath. Tears poured from his eyes, mixing with the blood from his nose and staining his muddy beard a watery pink color.

Tocho bent to help him, and Bader struck out with his foot, delivering a solid kick to the side of Tocho's head with his heavy work boot. Tocho dropped to the floor and lay there, unmoving.

"Alright, that's enough." Macalister turned to the door and stepped outside. "Four guards, around the clock. If they go to the shitter, they're manacled to a guard the whole time. Do I make myself clear?"

"Yes, boss." Morgan Gage stepped forward. "I'll see to it."

Macalister nodded curtly and walked back toward the front of the camp. This was unprecedented, and he wasn't sure what to make of it. Bob Taylor had to be lying. Dim-Corp was stingy with their DimGates, and nobody from IA would have one. Still, who else could they be? No one just walked up on this place. Suddenly, he stopped dead in his tracks. What if they were after the gold? He spun around, crashing into Bader.

"Goddammit, get out of the way." He shoved Bader aside and charged back around the corner.

"Open the fucking door, now."

The guard with the key quickly removed the padlock and chain, and opened the door as he stepped aside. Macalister stormed back in, followed closely by Bader. Bob and Tocho still lay on the floor where they had left them.

"Get him up on the box and wake him up," he ordered, kicking Bob in the ribs. "And don't fucking knock him out this time, I need answers from him."

"Sorry, boss." Bader heaved Bob up onto the box and slapped his cheeks until Bob focused on him. "Alright, he's awake."

Bader moved to the side, and Macalister stepped in close. He grabbed Bob by the throat and leaned in until their noses were almost touching.

"What the fuck were you looking for?"

Bob gagged and swatted feebly at Macalister's hand. Macalister relaxed his grip slightly, allowing Bob to suck in a wheezing gasp. He leaned back for a second, and with his free hand, he slapped Bob across the face, relishing the sting in his palm.

"What were you looking for?" he repeated, leaning back in close. "You better get straight with me real quick, or Bader is going to start carving pieces off your goddamn body."

"We were trying to see the layout of the camp," Bob whispered.

"Why? What were you planning? Were you going to steal from me?"

"No… just trying to see what you had going on here."

Macalister released Bob's throat with a shove and punched him in the eye. Pain shot up to his wrist from the impact, which helped to temper his rising panic. He took a moment to focus.

"You can drop the Internal Affairs act. We both know that's bullshit. Is there somebody else out there? Are you part of a group?"

Bob shook his head. "No group." He looked at Tocho lying on the floor. His eye was rapidly swelling up. He raised his hands in a gesture of defeat. "Okay, I give up. You've got me cold."

Macalister smiled grimly. His throbbing hand pulsed with every beat of his heart, but he never felt so completely alive as he did when he beat someone into submission.

"I'm just a business man," Bob said. "I'm from Europe. I'm over here looking for ways to get a trade route set up. You're kind of famous with the locals up north, with your chocolate. I was really just trying to check out your operation."

"So, you were trying to steal from me," Macalister said. "How did you know my name? And how did you know about the DimGate system?"

"You've got me all wrong," Bob protested. "The Aztecs told me about you, and I thought I might make a deal with you. Then, about two days north of here, I met some local tribe that told me you had a door that went to another world. They told me where your camp was, and that the door was in a big building in the middle. That's what I was trying to check out. I just wanted to see this door, and I panicked and told a lie when we got caught, and it snowballed into this."

Macalister relaxed a little. It sounded plausible, but then again, if he had talked to the Aztecs, then he might know about the gold. The DimGate was probably an interesting concept to a hick from an undeveloped dimension like this, but the gold, that would get anyone's attention. It didn't help that both of those things were in the warehouse. There were too many goddamn things happening at once, and he needed time to sort it all out. He turned and walked back out the door, ignoring the guards, and strode around the corner. Bader hurried to catch up.

"What do you think, boss?"

"I think things were better before the goddamn DimGate started working again."

They walked the rest of the way back to the office in silence.

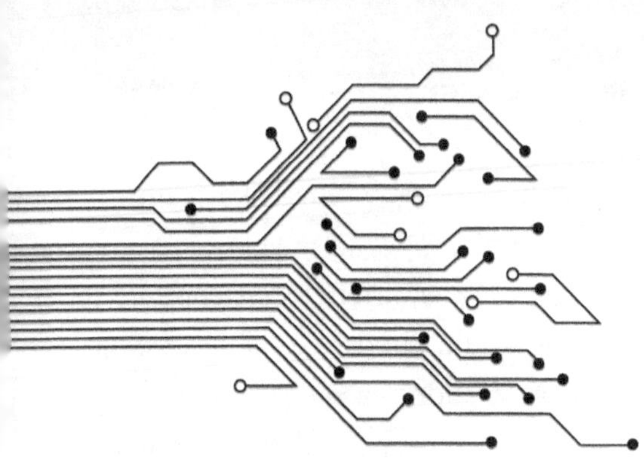

CHAPTER 11

Quentin stood before the elders, with his hands clasped before him to keep them from visibly shaking. The cooling-off period was over, and they were back in Viho's house to decide how they were going to handle the capture of Bob and Tocho. Quentin felt like he was on a stage in front of a crowd, even though there were only five people in the room. Public speaking was definitely not on his list of strengths. His mouth was dry, but he ignored it and focused on what he was about to say.

He looked around the room, making brief eye contact with each person, just as Eissa had coached him. Tahki and Viho sat on one side. Two of the tribe's elders sat on the other side, and Eissa was at the far end. She gave him an encouraging smile and a thumbs up, and he straightened his back.

"I spent a lot of time thinking about this today," he said. "I know you have, too. Bob and Tocho are important to all of us, and this is a very difficult position to be in."

Eissa subtly pointed to the left and the right, reminding him to sweep the room with his eyes, and avoid getting tunnel vision. He glanced around, grateful that they had worked on some public speaking tools. She had also told him to imagine that everyone in the audience was naked, but he decided that wasn't very sound advice, at least not in this situation. He resisted the urge to wipe the sweat off his forehead with his sleeve, and continued with his speech.

"It's not in the best interests of the Bribri to attempt a rescue for Bob and Tocho. That would almost certainly cost lives, and there's a good chance we wouldn't even be successful. There's also no way that Eissa and I can rescue them on our own. Rescue just isn't a good option."

Viho was nodding as he spoke, but Quentin didn't expect that to continue for long. He was just now getting to the controversial part.

"That being the case, I think we should go on with the original mission. If our plan works, and I believe it will, then we will be able to rescue Bob and Tocho once we have succeeded, or negotiate for their release. This way, the Bribri tribe will be reunited, the abuse by the guards will end, and Bob and Tocho will be released. It's the best way that I can think of to deal with this mess."

He looked at Tahki, trying to gauge her reaction. She nodded at him, her face neutral. It wasn't a standing ovation, but it wasn't an outright dismissal either, so he had that going for him. As always, Viho was a rock. It seemed that he only displayed anger and pain, and those only when they were boiling over.

"Please, sit," Tahki said, patting the rug beside her.

Quentin sat down quietly, surprised at how calm he felt. He was nervous, of course, but he wasn't the emotional train wreck he expected to be. Having Eissa there as an anchor made a big difference in his ability to stay calm, and he reminded himself to thank her later. She drove him crazy now and then, but he couldn't imagine trying to do this without her.

Tahki spoke up first. "You are wise for one so young. My heart is heavy with sadness for my friends, but they would be the first to say that we were fools for coming to get them. As to the mission, I am torn. I want my people to be one people, but I don't know if this is possible now. Macalister might have tortured Bob and Tocho for information and know our plans." She looked at Viho. "What do you think?"

"I am against all of this," Viho said, shaking his head slowly from side to side. "We have barely started down this road, and already it goes wrong. This is a sign that we should stop now. If we keep on, more of our people will be hurt or dead. No more. This must end now."

Quentin's face fell. There was no doubt that Viho was going to be against the idea, but with the elders nodding in agreement to what he said, it seemed that the tide was with Viho. What could he say to refute Viho's statement? It was all true, or at least plausible.

"That's bullshit," Eissa said, her voice low, but strong.

Quentin's eyes widened, and he swiveled his head to stare at her. He instantly knew that she was beyond angry. Her upper lip was curled in a snarl, and her eyes were black.

"Do you think that if you don't do anything, that everything will be okay? What do you think the DimCorp people are thinking right now? They just found two guys walking around in their camp. Do you think they're just going to write it off as two lost hikers?" She stared Viho down, her hands clenched into hard fists.

"Nobody in their right mind would sneak into that place unless they were planning something serious, and you can bet Vincent Macalister knows that. Right now, they're thinking that there's an army out here getting ready to attack them, because that's the only logical reason someone would be spying on them. If I were in their shoes, I'd try to beat them to the punch and attack first. For all we know, there might be a whole company of DimCorp soldiers headed for us right now. The time for cutting your losses has passed, Viho, and you need to face the truth and quit trying to quit."

Viho stood up, his whole body shaking with barely-controlled rage. He thrust a quivering finger at Eissa.

"What do you know about any of this? You are so quick to fight, to send us there to get killed. You told me you know my pain, but I wonder about that. Have you ever fought? Have you ever lost someone in a senseless battle?"

"I've seen more people get killed in a senseless war than you could even imagine," Eissa shouted, climbing to her feet. "I've had people bleed to death while I tried to keep their heart beating. I've held a man's guts in my hands, trying to keep them out of the mud, while he's begging me not to let him die. Don't you dare question me!"

"Enough," Tahki shouted. "Stop, both of you. Sit down." Her eyes blazed. "This is not how we talk to one another."

Quentin fought the overwhelming urge to run. He hated conflict under normal circumstances, but it was even worse here, when the stakes were so high. The anger in the room was like a rip current, and it was all he could do to keep his head above water. *You've got to get control of this, Quentin. Be a leader. You can do this.*

He scooted over and grabbed Eissa's hand. It was hot and rigid, but her fist slowly opened as she regained some of her composure. "Sit," he said softly. "Take a breath. It's okay."

Tahki was quietly coaching Viho in their native language, and Quentin took a deep breath. This meeting might have started off well, but it had spiraled out of control frighteningly fast. The emotions involved were powerful, and he had to be careful here. He didn't have any experience with fighting, or death, and trying to lead those who had been scarred by it was very touchy. It was a burden that he felt ill-prepared for a day ago, but now he was starting to realize just how incredibly unprepared he really was.

Eissa sat down, and Quentin continued to hold her hand. With each breath in the silence, he could feel her grip relaxing slightly. He glanced at Tahki, hoping she was going to take control of the meeting, but she was looking at Viho as she stroked his arm. They couldn't leave it like this indefinitely. Viho and Eissa had both said their piece, so the feelings were out in the open, but they still had to reach some sort of an agreement. He wished Bob were here to take over, and the irony of the thought brought a faint smile to his lips. At last, Quentin let go of Eissa's hand and stood up. Clearly, no one else was going to move things forward. It was up to him.

"Look, you both have valid points. This isn't a simple problem with a simple solution. We're all in this together, and Eissa's right, we can't just walk away now. Things have been set in motion, and there's no going back. We have to do something."

He looked at each of them, trying to find an ally. No one was looking at him, so he plunged on.

"Let's reason this out, put it all on the table. Bob and Tocho are prisoners in there. The only hope they have is for us to move forward with the plan. Even if we set that aside, moving forward with the plan is the only hope the Bribri people inside the plantation have. If we take away their hope, what will we leave them with? I don't know about you, but the idea of little kids growing up in that environment eats at me, some little girl watching her mom get whipped for working too slow. She'll grow up knowing her whole life is going to take place right there in that field, working and being punished, day after day. I can't walk away from that."

The room was silent.

"We have this one shot to change their future, to give them a reason for living. What do we gain by walking away? Our lives? Maybe. Will we sleep better knowing we didn't take a chance to help them? Will your heart rest easy if you had a chance but didn't try? Will you look back on this day with pride, or with regret?"

Tahki motioned for him to sit.

"Viho." She spoke softly, but with calm authority. Viho looked at her, then back at the floor.

"Viho, what does your heart say?"

Viho took a deep, shaky breath and let it out slowly. The weight of a mountain seemed to sit on his shoulders, an impossible load that was crushing him.

"I hate this decision." He looked up.

"But I hate that half my people are inside there, and now two more. I hate that more people are going to die, no matter what we do." He raised his hands in a gesture of surrender and let them fall to his lap. "My heart says to make it end."

He nodded to the two elderly men across from him. They whispered together for a moment.

"This is our heart, as well," the one on the left said.

Quentin felt a surge of hope lift him up. It was edged with doubt, but it was hope nonetheless, and he grasped it with all his strength. Somehow, they were going to do this, against all the odds. He squeezed Eissa's hand, and she squeezed back, a comforting gesture. The tension rolled off his shoulders in waves, leaving him almost giddy with relief.

Tahki stood. "Then this is what we must do. There is no disagreement among us. Tomorrow, we will gather the people and plan this out. Time is short."

The dew was still on the ground as Quentin and Mazik made their way down the trail beside the lake. Quentin wanted to scout out the trail and find a place to set up the ambush. The knowledge that he only had a day to put everything in place was in the front of his mind, chewing away at his nerves. When they reached the place where Mazik had found them, they turned and headed into the woods.

"How early do they usually come by?"

"They leave the camp at sunrise," Mazik said. "It will take them a half hour to get this far."

They passed by their DimGate a few minutes later. Quentin marveled at how well it blended into the forest around it. It was only a few feet away from the trail, but he almost walked by without seeing it.

Ten more minutes of fast walking brought them to a broad trail. Quentin looked up and down it, hoping to see something that would be helpful to them. To the north, the trail went straight for a while before bending out of sight to the right. To the south it was also straight, though it eventually dog-legged around a large tree and became obscured by its branches.

They turned right and walked south towards the tree. The jungle was thick on both sides of the trail, with evergreens and ferns competing for sunlight among the larger hardwoods. It was hard to see more than two feet off the trail, which surprised Quentin.

"It won't be as hard to hide people as I thought," he said. "The hard part will actually be getting them out of the woods and onto the trail."

"You don't want to be around the vines," Mazik said, pointing to a thick green cluster. "Poison Ivy."

They walked around the big tree in the middle of the trail, and Mazik nodded to a dense stand of evergreens about twenty feet back from the edge.

"This might work," he said. "It's open enough to do what we need to do. You can hide the archers between the trees, and the team to disarm and tie them up can hide behind them. It will still be dark in here that early, so that will help, and the evergreens won't make any noise when they move."

Quentin looked on the other side of the trail. There were a few large rocks scattered among the trees and vines on that side, but it looked almost impenetrable.

"We could put a few archers on that side," he said. "As long as they have a clear shot, they don't need to be able to run out onto the trail. I'll hide right here behind the tree, so I can just step out and stop them."

He tried to imagine what the moment of contact would be like, or, as his therapist would say, *visualizing your success.* Fifteen or twenty guys walking up the trail, while he stands behind this tree. He steps out, raises a hand, calls out to them. The slaves look up in surprise, then drop to the ground as the DimCorp guards start shooting…

He shook his head, trying to clear the image from his mind. Still, it wouldn't hurt to have a place to go, in case it went down like that. He looked around for a nearby rock or log to dive behind and started to step off the trail into the woods when Mazik stopped him.

"Don't. We can't leave tracks. We will have to leave the trail back there and come up through the jungle."

"Of course," Quentin said. He smacked himself on the forehead. "I'm a dumbass." He decided not to explain what he was looking for. Mazik wasn't the kind of guy who would appreciate a strong sense of self-preservation.

Mazik smiled. "We don't really need to go in there, anyway. This is a good place. We probably won't be able to use it twice, though. We need to go on down the trail and find another spot for the second ambush."

"Yeah, that's true. We'll have to leave them tied up right here by the trail. There's nowhere else to take them. That means we'll have to leave some people to guard them, too."

Quentin pulled out a notepad and pen, and made a quick sketch of the area. When he was done, they walked on down the trail. About ten minutes later, they came to another clearing. This one had evergreens on both sides, and was situated right after a turn in the trail.

"Oh, this is perfect," Mazik said. He spun in a circle. "There is a place for everyone here. Once we've taken them prisoner, we can keep them right here while we go to the DimCorp camp. This is good."

"Okay, so now we need to go back up and find a place to set up the triage center. Let me add this to my map real quick before we go."

"I think I know of a place for the triage center," Mazik said. "It's back up the trail the other way, just past where we came on."

Quentin put his notebook away, and it suddenly occurred to him that no one had pursued one of the points that Keme had made to Bob.

"You said that Keme thought Morgan Gage might agree to our terms, but that Macalister would not. Who is Morgan Gage?"

"He is the second in command, under Macalister."

"How come nobody's said anything about him?"

Mazik shrugged. "Because he has no power. Macalister doesn't share his power with anyone."

"So, do you think Macalister would send Gage with the second group of guards, or will he come himself? I didn't even think about what we do if Macalister shows up out here."

"Macalister won't leave the camp," Mazik said. "He is a coward. He is only tough when he can't be hurt."

"So, he would send Gage to be in charge of a battle?"

"Maybe. He might send Bader instead. Bader loves to fight."

"Who is he?"

"He is Macalister's puppet. His attack dog." Mazik spat in contempt. "He is strong, but he is stupid."

"Is Gage not as much of a fighter, then?"

"No, he is okay. He treats people with respect, mostly."

Quentin nodded. He was either going to stand in this clearing and face a rational human being who would engage in a discussion, or someone who would slit his throat without thinking about it. This new knowledge didn't do much to bolster his courage.

"Alright. We can only control what we can control. Let's go check out this triage site."

Mazik led the way back up the trail, passing the side trail that they had used to come up from the lake. When they arrived, Quentin saw that it was indeed a good spot. It was a small clearing, about a hundred yards across, and it was enclosed by jungle so dense that it couldn't be seen until you got to the opening.

"I like it," Quentin said. "It's close enough to the lake that we can haul water, and close enough to the ambush sites that we won't have to carry anyone too far."

"That covers everything we needed to find, right?"

"I think so," Quentin said. "Let's head back and get this thing organized."

"Everybody in the world hates mornings, but that's when everything gets scheduled," Eissa grumbled. "Why don't people schedule things for early afternoon?"

Quentin wrinkled his forehead in mock exasperation. "While you've been sleeping the day away, I already went out and recon'd the ambush sites, and we found you a great place for a triage center. We can take all your stuff up there today and get it ready. All you'll have to do in the morning is walk up there and hang out. That's not so bad, right?"

"At least I have a job," Eissa said. "I guess I should be happy I'm not in the same boat as Viho."

"Yeah, he didn't like the idea of staying at the triage center, did he?"

"It's hard being a celebrity," Eissa said. "You can't go places without causing a scene. I think he gets it, he just doesn't like it."

They watched as the archers practiced. A bundle of old clothes had been set up on a stump the approximate distance that they would be from the trail. None of them had missed it yet. After seeing all four of the archery squads hit the target, Quentin gathered them around him in a semicircle.

"Okay gang, this is the plan." He looked around the group, trying not to get hung up on how young some of them were, and drew a line in the dirt with a stick. "This is the trail. You'll be over here, hiding in the evergreens. The trade convoy will come up this way."

He pointed to the end of the line with his stick, and waited as they rearranged themselves so that everyone could see.

"Two of you will be assigned to each DimCorp guard. You are responsible for that guard, and no one else, unless it gets out of control, okay? That means that if the guy beside you shoots his guard, but your guard doesn't move, you don't shoot. You only watch your guard. Everybody got that?"

The archers nodded, murmuring their assent.

"I'm going to stop them, and do the talking. If everything goes right, you archers won't do anything at all, except watch. Once they lay down their guns, the restraint team will come out from behind you and tie them up. If one of them tries to use his gun, or make a run for it, the two men assigned to him shoot him. You'll have to make that decision yourselves. Is everyone good with that?"

More nods and grunts.

"I don't want anyone getting hurt, but if someone has to get hurt, let's make it them instead of us. Any questions?"

No one said anything. Quentin saw the eagerness in their faces, in their shining eyes, and he felt their excitement charging the air. He envied their carefree spirit, and their ability to ignore the fact that some of them might not be alive by this time tomorrow.

"Alright then. You guys pair up, and Mazik will assign everyone to their spot."

He turned away as Mazik took over, and walked back to where Eissa waited.

"Okay," he sighed. "I guess that went alright."

"They seem like they've got their shit together," Eissa said. "They're not all stressed out, anyway."

Quentin sighed. "The exuberance of youth. Most of them are too young to have any real concept of their own mortality. I could use some of that, myself. It'd probably make this whole thing easier."

"You're doing okay," Eissa said, grabbing his arm. "Let's go see how the rest of them are doing."

Beyond the archers, near the edge of the lake, a production line of sorts had been set up. The Bribri women had placed a bunch of stiff, dried rawhide skins in the lake the night before, weighing them down with rocks. Today, the hides were soaked through, making them manageable. They were carefully cutting them into strips and placing them in buckets of water to keep them pliable.

"Alright, everyone's doing their thing," Eissa said. "Now, let's find a quiet place and work on your speech."

Quentin nodded, and turned toward the trees at the edge of the village. This was the part that scared him the most. Not the guns that would likely be pointed at him, although that would be scary, too, but knowing that what he said would play a huge role in whether those guns got used or not. People's lives, DimCorp and Bribri alike, depended on what he said, and how he said it, and that was an incredible burden. He wished once again that Bob and Tocho were there.

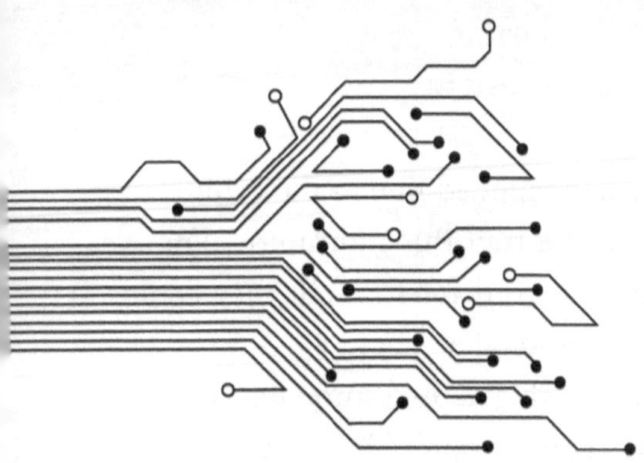

CHAPTER 12

Quentin sat on a bench in the village square, hunched over his notebook. The page was filled with scribbled notes and diagrams. No matter how he looked at it, he was a sitting duck in the ambush scenario. Once again, there was only one thing that could go right, and a thousand things that could go wrong.

"What's up?" Eissa stepped around the end of the bench and sat down beside him. "Do you have your speech memorized?"

He straightened up and tucked the notebook into his shirt pocket. "Mostly. I was just going over the ambush plan, trying to figure out how to make it safer."

Eissa grunted noncommittally.

There was a fine line between protecting her and lying to her, and Quentin had been getting closer and closer to it in the last few days. He didn't want her to worry about him and suffer an anxiety attack because of the additional stress. On the other hand, he was desperate to talk to someone about this, and she had been his confidant since they were riding tricycles together.

"Look, we both know I'm not cut out for the action hero bit." He glanced at her out of the corner of his eye as she snorted. "Thank you. Seriously, though, the plan is for me to step out from behind a tree and tell ten soldiers with machine guns to lay down their weapons. It sounded fine in the cabin, but when I stood out there on the trail this morning… I'm so vulnerable, there's not even a word for it. Hell, they could probably throw a rock at me and take me out."

Eissa grunted again, and they lapsed into silence for a few minutes. Quentin was about to pull his notebook back out of his pocket when Eissa jumped to her feet.

"Dude, we've got a fucking DimGate. Why don't we go to another dimension and get you a bulletproof vest or something?"

Quentin smacked himself in the forehead. "Idiot! Of course, we do. Why didn't I think of that?"

"It's because I'm the smart one, honey. You can't help it that you're a man. It's just the way the world works."

He raised an eyebrow but managed to avoid commenting. Instead, he climbed to his feet. "We've got to go right now if we're going to do this. Come on, I need your help."

"Do you want to tell Viho where we're going?"

He paused. Viho was against this whole thing to begin with. If they told him they were going to get Quentin a bulletproof vest, he would want them to get one for everyone. While that would be an understandable demand, it would also be almost impossible for them to produce in an hour.

"No, I think we're better off just doing it and not saying anything."

She nodded, and they began walking through the village towards the fields. Quentin silently berated himself for not considering the DimGate as a resource right away. They had the ability to travel anywhere, and they had a credit card with no limit. It was time to start thinking about that first, rather than at the last second.

"Where do you think we should go?" he asked, breaking the silence as they left the lake behind and entered the forest. "I don't even know how to go about buying this. You can't just go to a convenience store and grab one."

"Vegas, Dimension 443. We know the coordinates for the Diablo Tower, so we have a safe place to cross, and it's a really advanced dimension, so they probably have better technology in personal defense than anywhere else we might go."

Quentin nodded. "That's good thinking. My little man-brain probably wouldn't have been able to come up with that, either."

Eissa let out a rolling laugh and reached up and ruffled his hair. He ducked away with a chuckle and jogged a few steps to get away from her. Within minutes the door appeared, and Quentin opened the control panel.

He had a moment of panic when he reached in the cubby near the top of the panel where Bob kept the credit card stashed, and he didn't feel the card. He slid his fingers around, and finally found it back in the corner. With a sigh of relief, he slid it in his pocket and began programming the DimGate.

"Okay," he said, stepping back. "We're all set. Are you ready?"

Eissa nodded.

"Okay. I'll activate it, and you open the door a crack and peek through. We need to follow all the safety procedures, just like we would if Tocho and Bob were here."

She rolled her eyes and sighed dramatically. "Yeah, yeah, I know the drill. Push the button, Einstein."

Quentin activated the DimGate, and once it clicked, he gave Eissa a nod. She stepped around the corner, and he put his hand on the emergency stop button. She stood to the left of the door, leaned over, and cracked it open, and instantly the roar of the wind and the traffic assaulted them. Eissa pushed the door open the rest of the way, gesturing for him to follow. Quentin closed the panel and followed her through to the roof of the Diablo Tower.

The noise was incredible, compared to the silence of the Bribri village and the rain forest. Quentin fought the urge to cover his ears, and hoped they adjusted soon. The strobing billboards were a stark contrast to the green of the jungle, almost painful to look at.

"I forgot how intense this place is," he shouted.

"We were just here three days ago," Eissa said.

Quentin opened the panel and deactivated the DimGate. "I know, but a lot happened during those three days." He pulled a fuse and slipped it in his pocket before closing the panel. It was unlikely that anyone would come up here and mess with it, but it was always best to err on the side of caution.

They made their way over to the airlift. Quentin chuckled, thinking about their last trip down.

"Don't make fun of me," Eissa said. "I just don't like elevators that reach terminal velocity on the way down."

"I'm not laughing at you, I was actually laughing at myself. When we went down the other day, I wasn't holding on, and I floated most of the way down. I was just thinking about that."

Eissa looked at him suspiciously. "Uh huh. I want to believe you, but I'm struggling."

Quentin raised his hands in mock protest. "Honest injun, that's what I was thinking about."

Eissa's eyes widened in surprise. "You- you fucker! I can't believe you said that. I ought to kick your ass."

Quentin dropped to the ground, consumed with hysterical laughter. Eissa booted him in the ribs playfully, unable to keep from grinning. Quentin finally sat up, gasping for air. "Oh, man. That was some funny shit." He chuckled again as he wiped his eyes.

"It wasn't *that* funny," Eissa said. "I think you're having a nervous breakdown."

"Come on, I got you pretty good. I haven't pulled that one out in a long, long time." He climbed to his feet and brushed his pants off. "Whew! Okay, I think I'm alright."

"Well, at least you didn't follow it up with 'honest Native American' this time."

They laughed together at the memory. He had to admit, at least to himself, that he was acting rather giddy. It was probably a combination of the stress he was under, and nervousness about their current quest. Both things took him far away from his comfort zone. He took a deep breath in through his nose and let it out slowly. *Get yourself together, Q.* With one last glance back at the DimGate, he pushed the call button for the airlift.

He held on to the rail as they descended this time. The building wasn't that tall, at least, not compared to the skyscrapers around them, and it didn't seem like the lift could possibly pick up that much speed on the way down. He idly wondered, as his feet came off the floor, if it was propelled down instead of just using gravity. Eissa stared grimly out the window in silence, and a moment later they were on the ground level.

"Okay," Quentin said, guiding Eissa towards the street. "You made it. I guess we ought to get a cab, huh? What are we looking for? An army surplus store?"

Eissa nodded. "That's probably our best bet."

Quentin looked out over the traffic. The cars weren't like the cars he was used to. Most of them were autonomous and didn't even have steering wheels or drivers. How were you supposed to flag down a taxi with no driver? Especially one that was flying along a few stories up.

He turned to Eissa to point out the conundrum, but she was walking away from him. He caught up to her just as she approached the doorman of the Cosmos Kitchen. It was the same guy who had guided them in the previous weekend.

"Excuse me, sir," Eissa said. "Can you help us? We're trying to get a cab. Preferably, one that stays on the ground."

"Of course," he said. He took a few steps to his right and pushed a button on a pole near the curb. A yellow light began flashing on top of the pole, and an empty yellow car left the traffic lane and pulled up to the curb. The doorman opened the door for them. "Is there anything else I can help you with? Tickets? Recommendations?"

Quentin and Eissa exchanged a glance. "We're, uh, looking for a military surplus store," Quentin said. "Do you know of a good one?"

The doorman thought for a moment. "Well, I don't know if it's good or not, but there's a place out on the edge of town, big para-military place called Prepper's Paradise. You be careful, going to a place like that. Little bit scary, if you ask me."

"We'll be there and back before you know it," Quentin said. "We just need to run in. Thanks for the tip."

They climbed in the car, and the doorman closed the door. They sat there for a moment, looking around.

"How in the hell do you program this thing?" Quentin muttered. "There isn't even a screen."

A moment later the door opened, and the doorman stuck his head in. "Hello, taxi. Prepper's Paradise, please." He pointed at the white plastic square on the ceiling. "Swipe your card over that, and away you go." With a wink and a grin, he closed the door again, and the cab pulled away from the curb.

Prepper's Paradise was a massive compound. On the outside there were rows and rows of old military trucks, camouflage campers, deer stands, boats, and hovercraft. There was even a camouflage flying car on display floating ten feet off the ground.

"Must be hard to sell camo vehicles to passers-by," Quentin said. "You know, since no one can see them, and all." He laughed at his own joke, but Eissa merely rolled her eyes.

"Come on, funny man, let's get inside."

The taxi left as they made their way to the entrance. Inside they were greeted with racks of clothing. Across the store, signs hung from the ceiling indicating various departments such as guns, ammo, camping, shoes, personal defense, and survival.

"Jesus," Eissa muttered. "This place is the super Walmart for people with personality disorders."

Quentin stifled a laugh and pointed to the back-left corner. "Let's aim for the personal defense department, that sounds promising."

They passed a few other shoppers, and Quentin began to feel out of place. Everyone seemed to be wearing some sort of camo, and every man he saw had a beard. He was suddenly sure that his clean-shaven cheeks and button-down plaid shirt were broadcasting a message to everyone in the store that he was a geek, and not a prepper at all.

They passed the camping department, which had a mock campsite set up. Eissa stopped and pointed to the picnic table. "Dude, we totally need one of these." She picked up the box on the end of the table and read the label to him. "Repel-All, the leader in non-harmful insect and animal deterrents, emits an ultrasonic frequency guaranteed to keep everything from mosquitoes to bears at least fifty feet away."

Quentin chuckled. "I wonder if that works any better than the ones in our dimension. Have you ever read the reviews on these things?"

"No, why? Should I?"

"Oh yeah, great entertainment. People post pictures of roaches sitting on them, or mouse turds on them, that kind of stuff. It's a genius product idea, really. It doesn't have to do anything, and no one will ever know if it really works or not."

She set the box back on the picnic table with a sigh. "Alright, whatever, Mr. Moodkill. Let's go."

The personal defense department was huge. They passed a display case filled with stun guns, air horns, sprays, strobe lights, and things they had never seen before. Beyond that was a mannequin wearing a tactical vest, helmet, and goggles. Quentin paused to look at the vest, and a salesman approached them.

"Can I help you find something?" the man asked. He was wearing a black t-shirt with the Prepper's Paradise logo emblazoned across the front, and camo pants tucked into combat boots. His hair was shorter than Quentin's, buzzed almost to the skin, but his dark beard was massive.

"I'm looking for a bulletproof vest," Quentin said. He

realized he was staring at the tattoos on the salesman's knuckles, and hurriedly glanced up at his face. "Do you sell those here?"

"Got the biggest selection in the country. Do you know what you want?"

Quentin shrugged. "Not really, no. What are the options?"

"Let's start with the basics. Come on back, we'll get it narrowed down. My name's Jake, by the way." He led the way past the gas masks. "Do you want to wear it under your shirt so no one can see it, or on top, like a full tactical vest?"

"Under would be great," Quentin said. "I didn't even know that was an option."

"Oh, sure. We've got Ultra-Thins that aren't any thicker than a sweatshirt. Now then, what are you protecting against? Bullet, laser, knife, needle?"

"Needle?" Quentin's eyebrows rose in surprise. "Like, flu shot needle?"

Jake laughed. "Like dirty heroin needle that's been coated in shit in a prison toilet. If you're a prison guard, that's a real threat. I'm guessing that's not you."

Quentin flushed. "No, definitely not me. Bullets are my main concern."

"Alright, I hear you. Handguns?"

Quentin paused. He had no idea what the DimCorp guards would be carrying. "I don't really know. They might be carrying machine guns."

Jake gave Quentin an appraising look. "You're messing with some bad dudes, huh? Alright, let's try the Ultra-Thin 3DX. It's a gel-spun fiber weave, good for most things short of a sniper rifle. Weighs under two kilos, protection all the way around the torso."

He pulled a white vest off the hanging rack and held it up in front of Quentin, then put it back and pulled a different one out. "Here, let's try this one on."

Quentin slid the vest over his head, surprised at how little it weighed. Even through his shirt, he could tell the lining was soft and cushioned. Jake helped him adjust the Velcro straps on the shoulders and the sides, then stood back.

"Are you sure this thing is bulletproof? It doesn't seem like there's anything to it." Quentin patted his stomach. "I mean, it feels good, it just doesn't seem like it could stop a bullet. I thought it would have a big metal plate or something."

Jake took a step back and pulled a pistol out of a holster on the inside of the waistline of his pants. He pulled the slide back and released it as he turned to one side, and pointed it at Quentin, spreading his legs in a shooter's stance. "Let's find out, what do you say?"

Quentin's eyes bulged, and he threw his hands in the air. "What? No! No, let's not find out, what's wrong with you?"

Jake burst out laughing and slid the gun back in the holster. "I'm just messing with you, man. It's cool. How's the vest feel? Good range of motion?"

Quentin lowered his arms, his face burning. "Yeah, it seems to be fine." He looked around for Eissa, but she was looking at the tasers and hadn't even seen what just happened. Maybe that was for the best. At least she couldn't give him shit about getting punked at the prepper store.

Jake began releasing the straps and lifted the vest off, setting it on the counter. "What else are you looking for? I saw your friend looking at the stun guns. Do you need a non-lethal weapon? We've got a lot of options there, like sonic weapons, high-voltage incapacitators, non-lethal pro-jectiles for firearms, all kinds of stuff."

It was a tough question, and Quentin didn't have an answer right away. Did it make sense to carry something non-lethal into a gunfight? Maybe, since diplomacy was still his goal. But how willing would someone be to compromise if they'd been tased, or shot with a bean bag? And how trustworthy?

Eissa wandered back over, grinning from ear to ear. "Dude, you gotta come see this. They've got a thing that supposedly protects you from psychic intrusion."

Quentin chuckled. "Nice to know there are loonies here, too." It occurred to him then that Jake was still standing there, and he wiped the grin off his face and glanced around. "No offense meant, if you're into that kind of thing."

Jake winked. "Nah, man, it's cool. That bullshit appeals to some people, and if they want to buy it, we'll sell it to them. But if you want to see the really cool stuff, it's over in the wearables."

Intrigued, Quentin shrugged. "Sure, we'll take a quick look, but we need to get back pretty soon."

Jake led them around the corner and over a few aisles. The two orange and gray exoskeletons on display dominated the area. They were external frames, rather than a fully-en-closed Iron Man suit, but there was no mistaking them for anything else. Quentin walked over to the nearest one, his heart pounding.

"Is this what I think it is?"

Jake laughed. "Yeah man, that's the new PRX 60. If you strap yourself in that bad boy, you can run 30 kilometers an hour, pick up five hundred kilos, vertical jump over three meters, and maintain a 200 gig per second data connection to the cloud. It's got a full heads-up display in the visor, shows you everything going on around you in a 300-meter radius, hyper-speed video upload for live-action gaming, everything. Of course, you can't buy weapons for them since they're civilian models, but if you know what you're doing, that won't slow you down."

For the first time since they left the island, Quentin completely forgot about everything that was going on. The sheer thrill of seeing something this awesome blocked out all the stress and worry. He reached out a hand and touched it, savoring the cold of the metal as he imagined himself walking down the street in it.

"I don't know what I'd do with it, but I want one so bad I can't stand it," Eissa said, grinning.

Quentin nodded in agreement. "You and me both. Live-action gaming in that thing? Yes, please!"

"$39,999 and it's yours," Jake said. "No one else in town has this model yet."

"Well, maybe some other time. We've got a rather pressing situation to deal with right now."

Jake turned them around to the display case on the opposite side of the aisle. "I hear you, man. If the Exo's are a bit too flashy for you, we've got a full line of micro movers. These are a lot like your household Thought-Pro logistics management systems. Some of them are even made by the same people, but instead of reading your brainwaves for lighting and climate control commands, or changing the channel, these allow you to move small objects remotely."

He unlocked a drawer and pulled out two black wrist-watches and turned back to Quentin. "Let's put one of these on each wrist, and you can try it out. It'll only take a second."

Once they were securely strapped to Quentin's wrists, he could see they weren't watches at all. They each had a series of numbers on the display, but it wasn't the time. Jake pointed to a bowling ball on the floor near the exoskeletons.

"Alright, buddy. Imagine picking that ball up and moving it over a few feet."

Quentin was suspicious that Jake was putting him on, trying to make a fool of him again. On the other hand, they obviously had some technology here that hadn't made it to his dimension yet, and if this was legit, the implications were huge.

He looked at the bowling ball and focused on lifting it up. Instantly, the ball rose two feet into the air. The wrist bands became warm against his skin, but not hot enough to burn. Quentin was so surprised that he stopped focusing on holding it there, and the ball crashed back to the rubber mat. Eissa gasped, and he tried again. This time he was ready, and when the ball was in the air, he willed it to move across the center display area and back. The further away the ball got, the harder it was to control, and the hotter the wrist bands became. Jerkily, he brought the ball back to the rubber mat and lowered it gently back to the floor.

"That's fucking incredible," Quentin whispered. "What are the limitations on weight and distance? How long does it hold a charge?"

"It's pulling power from you, so it doesn't need an external source. The range is subjective, it all depends on how heavy the object is, and how hard you're focusing. The same with weight, really. You can move bigger stuff, like fifty kilos, but you need to be pretty close to it. The lighter the object, the further away it can be. You noticed that the bowling ball got hard to hold steady on the other side of the aisle, right? You get a feel for what you can do with it with some practice."

Quentin looked at Eissa, then back to Jake. "I'll take it. These and the vest."

Jake smiled, although it didn't reach his eyes. "The micro movers are $6,499. Is that going to be a problem?"

Quentin met his stare. "My employer has deep pockets. And he's feeling very generous today." He handed Jake the credit card. "I won't need a bag, I'll just wear my purchases."

"Hey man, I just had to make sure you had the bills. Lots of people like the tech toys, but they can't afford to play." He led them back to the counter where they left the vest.

While Jake rang up the purchase, Quentin slipped out of his shirt and put the vest on. Eissa helped him with the straps, snugging it up to his ribs. He slipped his shirt back on and signed an illegible scrawl on the checkout screen, and a minute later, they were walking out the front door.

•————○

Quentin stared out the window of the taxi. The sense of elation hadn't left him yet, though he knew it would turn back into dread once they got back to the village. He watched the tower of cars flying above him, marveling once again at the incredible technology in this dimension.

"I gotta say, Prepper's Paradise wasn't as bad as I thought it would be," he said, turning to Eissa, who sat across from him in the rear-facing front seat. "I was nervous going in, but that place has got some really cool shit."

Eissa grinned. "Oh, it was bad, they just had enough interesting stuff to make it bearable. And it wasn't full of customers, that would have made it a lot worse. The people are the problem in places like that."

Quentin thought about Jake drawing a gun on him but decided not to mention it. Eissa would either give him shit about it, or she would turn the cab around and go kick Jake's ass on Quentin's behalf, and it was a tough call on which would be worse. He shifted, still trying to get used to the squeezing sensation of the vest. It was strangely comforting, he couldn't deny that, but it was mildly cumbersome at the same time.

"Seeing all those non-lethal weapons really made me think twice about our approach to this whole mission," Quentin said. "The vest makes me feel a lot better about things, but if bullets start flying for real, it would be good to have a way to shut everyone down with a sonic weapon or something."

"Why didn't you get one?"

"A couple of reasons. One, if the guards start shooting, the archers will kill them before I could even react. Two, a sonic weapon would affect everyone, including us, which would suck. Three, I need them to negotiate from a position of empowerment, not disempowerment."

Eissa nodded. "Well, I'm glad we got you a vest. I don't think you could kill anyone, so a gun would have been pointless, but at least you're protected from someone shooting you."

"Or stabbing me with a knife, sword, laser, or dirty heroin needle." Quentin chuckled. "There's apparently way more to attacking people than I ever knew."

Eissa smirked. "Well, you're about to get a graduate degree in attacking people. If shit goes south when you confront them, you're going to learn all kinds of things you didn't know."

The taxi swerved over to the edge of the road and stopped. Quentin looked out the window in surprise. They weren't even on the Strip yet, so they shouldn't be stopping. They were in front of a tire shop, and the high-rise casinos and hotels were visible behind it, a few blocks away.

"What's going on?" Eissa asked.

"*Attention, please.*" A robotic female voice came from the car's speakers. "*Attention. It sounds like you might be a perpetrator or victim of violent crime. Please wait until law enforcement officials arrive to assist you.*"

Quentin and Eissa stared at one another in confusion.

"What?" Quentin managed.

The car repeated the message.

"No, no, everything is fine. Please take us to the Diablo Tower."

"*You are being detained for law enforcement officials,*" the voice stated. "*Please stay inside the vehicle.*"

Eissa reached for the door handle, but it was locked. The window wouldn't go down, either. Quentin tried the door on the other side, but it wouldn't budge. They were trapped.

"Dude, this is not cool," Eissa said. "We don't have time to deal with the police. We don't even have an ID card for this dimension."

Quentin's heart skipped a beat. "Shit. We gotta get out of here." He leaned back and kicked at the window. His boots bounced off, leaving smudges on the glass, but no cracks. The panic of claustrophobia crept into the corner of his consciousness. He looked around the car for something, anything, to bludgeon the windows out. There was nothing inside the car, of course.

"Shit!" he cried out in frustration. "Shit, shit, shit." Rage was a welcome alternative to claustrophobic panic, and he raised his fist to punch the window. As his hand neared his face, he faintly registered the black band on his wrist. A surge of hope shot through him. "The micro mover! Of course!"

Eissa stared at him in confusion, but he closed his eyes, blocking out the distractions. He focused all his energy on imagining himself opening the taxi door from the outside. He cracked an eye open, but the door remained closed.

"Push on the door," he said through gritted teeth. "I'm trying to lift the handle."

Eissa pushed on the door as he focused his effort. "It's not moving," she said.

A siren wailed in the distance, and panic set in. Quentin abandoned the door handle, and instead imagined himself turning into the Incredible Hulk and ripping the door off the car. Every ounce of energy he had went into the visualization, and he trembled from the mental exertion. The car shifted, and the roof buckled slightly inward over Eissa's head. She shrieked as the door began to slowly peel away from the car at the bottom. Quentin squeezed his eyes closed and screamed in an adrenaline-infused rage, his hands clawing the air in front of him. The wrist bands burned his arms like molten metal, but he barely felt the pain. At last, the latch broke with a loud bang, and the door tore itself off the hinges and fell onto the sidewalk with a crash of shattered glass.

"Holy fucking mother of pearl," Eissa breathed. "What the hell did you just do?"

Quentin hurled himself out of the car and reached back in to grab her arm. "Come on, we've got to go."

She clambered out of the wrecked cab, and they turned to see a group of mechanics standing in front of the open bay doors, staring at them in shock. The sirens were close now, coming from somewhere above them. He pulled her down the sidewalk, breaking into a trot.

"Don't look up," he said. "They've probably got video cameras everywhere."

Quentin kept his head down and turned the corner at the first intersection they came to. A group of people were coming out of a souvenir shop, and he slowed to a walk and joined in the back of the crowd as they moved down the street. Behind them, the siren cut off, and he assumed the police had arrived at the wrecked taxi. He cast a furtive glance over his shoulder, but there was no one there except an elderly couple coming out of the coffee shop across the street.

"Oh my God," Eissa gasped. "Look at your arms."

"What?" Quentin raised his hands, perplexed. The skin around the wrist bands was red and blistered. "Oh. Oh, damn, that's going to hurt."

"Is that from using the mover things to rip the car door off?"

He nodded. "Yeah. I probably exceeded the manufacturer's recommended exertion a bit. It gets hot when you overuse it."

"Ya think?" Eissa shook her head. "I've got some burn cream in my aid bag. Remind me when we get back. If we get back."

Quentin nodded. "We're getting back, don't worry. We just have to hoof it."

There didn't seem to be an immediate pursuit, so they crossed the street and left the group behind. Two more turns had them on the Strip, but they were at least a mile from the Diablo Tower. They had no choice but to walk all the way. They didn't know enough about this dimension to know if it was safe to take another cab, or if the cab would recognize them or their credit card and call the cops again. It seemed unlikely, but there was no way Quentin was going to risk it.

They maintained a fast walk, threading their way through knots of slow-moving tourists. Some of the casinos were the same in this dimension as they were in Quentin's home dimension, which came as a surprise. They passed the impossibly tall Stratosphere tower, the Luxor pyramid, New York, New York, and Caesar's Palace.

"It's crazy that it's the same as our dimension," Quentin said. "Or, you know, similar."

"Did you notice that there was no Statue of Liberty at New York, New York?" Eissa asked.

"Hhmmm," Quentin grunted. "Interesting." He tried to remember the circumstances surrounding the creation of the statue, but other than being a gift from France in the late 1800's, he couldn't come up with anything. A siren up ahead jarred his thoughts, and he froze for a moment.

"It's not us," Eissa said. "Looks like a fender bender. Come on."

At last, hot and sweaty from the exertion, they arrived at the entrance to the Cosmos Kitchen. The doorman gave them a smile and a wave as they walked past.

"All good?" he called across the sidewalk.

Quentin patted his chest with a grin. "All good."

They entered the airlift and rocketed to the roof. The DimGate sat there waiting, just as they left it, silent in the ever-present roar of wind and traffic.

"I can't believe I'm saying this," Eissa said, "but I'm sort of relieved to be crossing back to the Bribri's dimension. Two hours here pretty much finished me off this time."

Quentin opened the control panel nodded with a wry grin. "I know what you mean. We gotta learn to keep our damn mouths shut when we're in this dimension. Big Brother listens to your conversations. That's kind of scary."

"Kind of?" Eissa arched her eyebrows. "That's like saying Hitler was kind of an asshole."

Quentin activated the DimGate and closed the control panel. "You know what I mean. Let's get back to the village and find your burn cream. My wrists hurt like hell."

It was a strange sensation to be afraid of this place. Up until today, it had been the beacon of excitement and the source of supplies for them. Now there was a small dark stain on it, a glimpse behind the curtain that revealed more than they had bargained for. On the upside, his impulse buy of the micro movers was now justified. He also knew what they were capable of, and the price he would pay for pushing the limits. His wrists were chafing and sore under the bands, but it was a whole lot better than sitting in a police station trying to explain who they were.

Quentin smiled as he opened the door to the relative silence and humidity of the rain forest on the other side, imagining what Tocho and Bob would think about him ripping a taxi door off with his brain waves. The smile was short-lived, though, as the reality of the situation came crashing back. At this point, the most he could do was hope that Bob and Tocho were still alive, and still in this dimension.

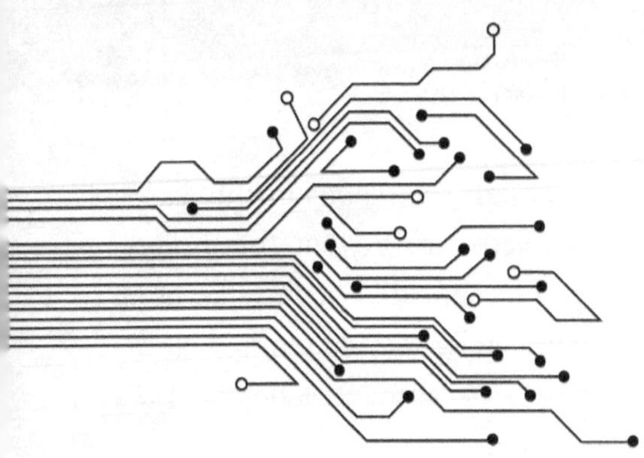

CHAPTER 13

Quentin woke up with a start, unsure of where he was. He rubbed the sleep from his eyes.

"It's time," Mazik said, barely visible in the darkness. He stood and walked to the table, where a low candle burned.

Quentin dressed in the relative darkness, fumbling with the straps on the vest, and shook Eissa before applying burn cream to his throbbing wrists. She stuck one hand out from under the blanket and flipped him the bird.

"Go away, unless you have coffee and a damn good excuse." She pulled the blanket over her head, muffling her voice. "On second thought, go away, even if you do."

"I hear you," Quentin said. "I woke up every hour, all night long, worrying about oversleeping, or forgetting something important. I'm exhausted."

Eissa sat up, her hair sticking out in every direction. She looked like a little kid pouting, and he laughed.

"Now that's a look. No wonder you can't get women to come back a second time."

"Fuck off. What's for breakfast, Mazik?"

"Leftover stew and cornbread. Come get it while it's hot."

They ate quickly. When they got outside, a silent group of grim men and women were gathering in the square. The moon was bright, and Quentin was grateful to have it. It was still going to be hard to get through the woods in the dark and get everyone where they needed to be, but the moon would be a tremendous help. He chuckled at how accustomed he was to things like artificial lights, and remembered a line from an Edward Abbey book about the beam of a flashlight being a prison for the eyes.

He glanced around, and located Viho at the center of the group. Moving carefully through the crowd, he put his hand on Viho's shoulder as he walked up. "Do we have everyone?"

"Waiting on two more."

Quentin took a step back and cleared his throat. "Can everyone hear me?"

The group of men and women gathered around him in a circle. "Okay, let's do a quick equipment check. I know it sounds silly, but does everyone have their bows and arrows?"

A murmur of assent rippled around the group.

"Archers. Does everyone know what team they're on? Left side of the trail, right side of the trail?"

More grunts and nods.

"Disarm and restraint team, I know your buckets are already up there, but just remember to pick up all the weapons and centralize them away from the guards, and double check each other. We don't want anyone to get hurt because we overlooked something. Also, remember to stay out of the archer's line of fire as best as you can."

He looked around the group.

"Does anyone have any questions?"

No one said anything. Viho stepped forward, looking over the group.

"No matter what happens today, I am proud of the

Bribri people. You have suffered much in your lives, but you still have courage and hope. I am Viho, and you are welcome in my home."

He walked off towards the trail by the lake, and they all fell in behind. They moved quickly and quietly, and as they entered the forest, Quentin struggled to keep up. The challenge of the dark trail kept his mind from wandering, and before he knew it, they were at the triage center.

Eissa wrapped her arms around him, pulling him down into a tight hug.

"You are a fucking rock star, Quentin," she whispered fiercely. "You go do this, and fucking own it. I'll see you when it's over."

"Thank you," Quentin said. Burning tears were welling up in his eyes, and he steeled himself against it. "Just in ca-"

"Nope, don't say that, don't even think it," she cut him off. "Focus on what you're going to say down there, and remember the delivery. It's all about how you say it."

She released him and stepped back, wiping her eyes. "Go on."

Viho stepped up and gripped his forearm. His fiery gaze burned into Quentin as he squeezed. The pain in Quentin's wrist from Viho's grasp shot to his shoulder, but he clamped down on the urge to scream. After a moment, Viho released Quentin's arm and turned away in silence.

Quentin stepped back out onto the trail, checking for the thousandth time that he was wearing the vest, and that he had the micro movers strapped securely to his forearms above the burns. The line of silent men formed up behind him as he found Mazik.

"Ready?"

He nodded. Mazik set off at a fast clip. Quentin practiced his lines as he walked. He pictured himself in a movie, and tried to become the character he imagined for this role; someone tough and determined, the kind of guy that could intimidate you with a look. Sometimes Eissa had some genius ideas, and he decided that this was one of those times.

The clearing gleamed in the moonlight beyond the tree in the trail. The break in the jungle canopy provided a distinct contrast, and the trail glowed white, an iridescent strip against the dark forest. As Quentin looked up at the sky, he realized with surprise that it was getting lighter. It was still black under the trees, but the stars were beginning to fade.

Quentin stood by the tree as Mazik directed the archers. They melted into the darkness to take their positions. He heard the rustle of leaves here and there, but he couldn't see anyone. To his right, a small branch cracked, and then another, as the archers tried to improve their fire lanes. After a few minutes the silence was complete, and Quentin was all alone.

He was watching the last of the stars fade away, hoping to see a meteor, when he heard a sound in the distance. He peered around the tree. The trail was becoming more visible on the other side of the clearing. There wasn't anything in sight. He relaxed. It might have come from one of the Bribri.

He looked around the clearing, trying to find any sign of the archers. Despite the fact that he could see fairly well, and knew there were people there, he could see nothing that stuck out from the forest. Just as he pulled his head back around the tree, he heard the sound again, this time closer. It sounded like singing, but it was too faint and broken to tell.

Mazik materialized beside him, and his heart surged, dumping adrenaline into his system.

"You scared the shit out of me," he breathed, clapping his hand to his chest.

"They're coming," Mazik whispered. "The slaves are singing."

Quentin stood there for a moment, shaking uncontrollably.

"Are you okay?" Mazik asked.

"Yeah, just my nerves. I'll be okay."

Mazik nodded, and faded back into the forest gloom.

Quentin focused on breathing normally for a minute. When his heart slowed down, he peered around the edge of the tree. He could just make out movement, at the very edge of his visibility range. He straightened, closed his eyes, and got back into character.

The singing got louder, and he was able to track their progress without giving himself away by looking around the tree repeatedly. When they entered the clearing, he took a deep breath and readied himself to step out onto the trail. Suddenly a voice rang out.

"Whoa, hold up, hold up. Let's take a piss break. Two minutes boys, two-minute break."

Quentin froze. This was a stroke of luck, but it could also go horribly wrong if they stepped off the trail too far to pee. All it took was one guy going into the trees to ruin the plan. He had to act now.

He stepped out onto the trail. The group stretched halfway across the clearing. The guards at the front were only ten feet away from him, and all three had their rifles slung over their shoulders and were opening their flies when he called out.

"Good morning."

The guard's heads swiveled towards him in unison, as did several of the slaves. Further down the line people were still talking and laughing, and he realized that only the ones up front knew he was there.

The guard closest to him grabbed for his rifle.

"Stop right there," Quentin shouted, extending his arms out, palms facing the guards. "Nobody move a muscle. Do you hear me? Any man who touches his gun dies instantly. No one moves, and everybody will live."

The guards glanced at one another in the sudden silence. The guards from the middle of the group stepped out to the side of the trail, trying to see what was going on.

"What the fuck's going on up there?" someone shouted from the back.

Quentin was not in the best position to control the situation. He stepped off the trail a few feet, still holding out his hands.

"Listen up," he yelled. "You in the back, step over here where you can hear me. Keep your hands away from your guns, and listen to me. If you touch your gun, you will die, no second chances. Can everyone hear me?"

One of the guards in the middle group stepped forward, unslinging his rifle. "Who the-"

Two arrows appeared in his chest, driving him backwards. A third went through his mouth and stuck out the back of his head. He fell to his knees with a look of confusion, dropping his rifle.

"Nobody else touch their fucking gun," Quentin roared. "You are surrounded, and you will die just like he did. Don't touch your guns."

He couldn't see what happened in the back, but another man fell to the ground. He fired his rifle as he fell, and two more arrows thudded into his chest. Quentin's ears were ringing, and someone was screaming in the trees, but he barely noticed as he charged down the side of the trail.

"Nobody fucking move," he screamed. "How many of you have to die before you just freeze? Goddammit, don't be so fucking stupid. Who's in charge here?"

One of the men nodded towards the body on the ground.

"Oh, that's great. Fucking great." He realized that he was on the verge of losing control of his temper. His hands were clenched into tight fists, and he forced his fingers out straight.

He glared up and down the line, furious that his no-injuries, no-deaths plan was falling apart. No one else was moving. "Alright, everyone, hands straight up in the air. Now. If you touch your fucking gun, you will die. Hands up."

Hands went up all down the line.

"Slaves, take two steps to the other side of the trail, and sit down. Do it now."

As the slaves were stepping back, another guard at the back of the line grabbed for his gun. He dove off the trail at the same time, rolling toward the trees. He popped up on his knees, opening fire into the evergreens. Arrows slammed into him from both sides, and he fell to the ground. Smoke hung over the clearing.

Quentin raced over to the fallen guard and picked up his rifle. "Does anyone else not believe me? Oh my God, I can't believe this is happening. What the fuck is wrong with you people?"

He stood there beside the fallen guard, pointing the rifle at the remaining guards at the end of the line. "Disarmers," he shouted.

The Bribri came out of the woods like ghosts with their buckets, and approached the line.

"Keep your hands in the air, and don't move a muscle," Quentin shouted. "No one else needs to die today. These men are going to take your weapons, and tie your hands behind your back. If you comply, you will not be harmed, and you will be returned to DimCorp. If you resist, you will die like these fucking idiots." He kicked the dead guard beside him.

The disarming crew worked quickly. They searched each guard, and collected a variety of handguns and knives, in addition to the rifles. Once they were all restrained, Quentin directed them to the trail.

"Mazik, take over the guards," he called. "I gotta see what our injuries are."

As Mazik called the archers out to control the guards, Quentin ran towards the tree line.

"Who's hurt?" he called, forcing his way through the branches.

"Over here."

He burst out the other side, and his stomach dropped. Two Bribri sat there covered in blood, and a third lay prone, obviously dead.

"Medical transport team," he shouted. "Three for transport, right now."

Burning rage boiled inside him as he pulled bandages out of his pocket and quickly wrapped the bullet wounds of the injured men. It wasn't supposed to be like this. No one was supposed to get hurt. All they had to do was listen, and none of this would have happened.

He fought the doubt that was creeping in, doubt with an insistent, convincing voice that was telling him that his plan wasn't working, that he was making things worse. Just knowing that Viho was waiting at the triage center was enough to make him want to throw up. They had undoubtedly heard the gunfire and knew that things were going wrong. He shook his head, forcing himself to focus on the injured men in front of him.

"Hang on guys," he said. "We're going to get you taken care of."

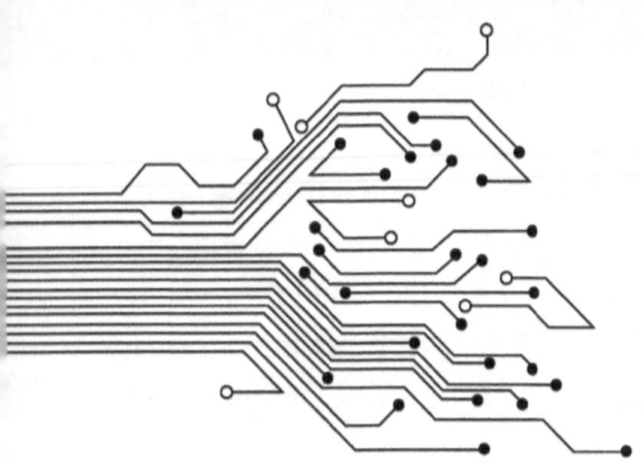

CHAPTER 14

The men who had disarmed the guards transitioned into their next role and raced back into the woods. They retrieved the makeshift stretchers they had stashed away from the trail, and loaded the two wounded men and the dead man.

"Let's get those guards loaded up too," Quentin directed. "I want all of them to be checked out by Eissa. Let's move, these guys need help fast."

"We don't have enough litters to carry them all," said one of the Bribri men.

"Well, we'll just have to come back and get the Dim-Corp guys," Quentin said as he lifted the back end of a litter. "Let's go, quick as you can."

They made their way around the end of the clump of trees, and over to the trail. It was full light by this time, which made finding their way over the fallen branches while carrying the wounded a little easier. Once they were on the trail, they moved quickly.

Quentin looked down at the man he was carrying, and realized that he had the dead one. His stomach took a hard roll, and he gritted his teeth and squeezed his throat shut, determined not to vomit. He looked up at the sky, breathing through his nose, and counted his steps to distract himself.

Once he felt like his stomach was under control, he made himself look back down at the body.

He couldn't be sure, but it looked like one of the young men from Mazik's little troop. A boy, really. If he had been in a different dimension, he'd be fresh out of high school. His next thought almost made him cry: thousands of boys fresh out of high school get killed in wars, even in first-world countries. Maybe especially in first-world countries.

His face was clear, but his bare chest was an unrecognizable mass of bloody flesh. A bullet had clearly hit him from the side and come out the front. His whole body jiggled as they carried him. Quentin wished that it wouldn't.

His arms were burning from the weight of the litter, and he welcomed the pain. At least it was something physical that he could focus on. The idea that he wanted to punish himself for not preventing this crossed his mind, but he dismissed it. The mental pain was far worse; it wasn't going to stop when he laid this kid down. It would probably get worse.

At last, they passed the small trail the led down to the lake, and a moment later they turned into the clearing where the triage center was set up.

"I've got a couple of wounded Bribri, and one that's dead," he called to Eissa. "Where do you want us?"

"Live over here, dead over there," she directed. "Space them out for me, I need room to work. Are they all gunshot wounds?"

"Yeah, all bullet wounds. I put a field dressing on them to try to slow down the bleeding."

"Okay, good. I'll take it from here."

Quentin rubbed his arms and flexed his hands for a moment, trying to get the circulation back. He stepped away as Viho approached; he wasn't ready to deal with Viho's grief and anger yet. He had to get himself together and prepare for the next ambush. The sudden realization that he had to do all of this again hit him hard, and it took a moment to realize that Eissa was shouting at him.

"Quentin, I need some help."

He turned and jogged over to her. "What can I do?"

"This guy got hit in the brachial artery. He needs surgery, like, right now."

She packed the hole in his bicep, and grabbed the hand of one of her assistants and placed it on top of the wound.

"Keep your hand on that, firm pressure. Don't let off of it, or he'll bleed to death." She turned to Quentin. "This is way beyond what I can do. He needs someone to sew his artery back together."

"Can't you do that?"

"No, you gotta have another piece of artery to put in there, like replacing a section of pipe."

"We don't have anywhere to take him," Quentin said. "What does that leave us for options?"

"He's got about fifteen minutes," Eissa said. "I guess the only thing we can do to keep him alive is to cauterize it."

Quentin's mind was racing as he considered all the angles. "We'll never get a fire built and hot enough that fast, and we can't get him to the village that fast, either."

"My other option is to amputate his arm, but I really don't have the tools for that, either. Also, we'd still need to do some cauterizing."

"The cabin," Quentin said. "There's a little propane torch at the cabin. It's in the box of tools on the porch."

"Can you get there and back?"

"The door is right around the corner," Quentin said, already running. "I'll be right back."

"Bring a screwdriver or something," Eissa shouted after him. "Something metal, with a handle."

He waved his hand, and raced out onto the trail. He watched carefully for the door as he ran, knowing that he didn't have time to run past it. His eyes scanned the trees, watching for a shape that didn't fit. After a minute of running, he saw the door and skidded to a stop. He opened the panel on the side and input the dimension information for the island.

He reached for the switch to activate the door. His hand faltered, and he stared at the screen. A small voice, deep in his mind, whispered that he could change the destination dimension. All he had to do was change that little number on the screen, and step through the door to his own world and escape from all of this. No more death and destruction, no more stress, he could just walk away. It had been over a month, so he could probably cross right into his apartment safely, and just leave all this behind. No one would ever know.

He thought about the dead people lying in the meadow, and the guys back at the ambush site waiting to fight again. How many of them would be dead when this was over? All because of him? And how was he going to face Viho, who knew this would happen? His fingers touched the screen, activating the dimension selection field. Almost in a trance, he changed the number to 165.

The panel hummed, and the door clicked. He wasn't even aware of hitting the button, but his heart was beating a hole in his chest as he realized that home was on the other side of the door, just inches away. He could even tell where the door would put him. He zoomed in the map on the bottom of the screen, and moved it around until he found his apartment. The panel hummed again. He decided to just crack the door open and peek for a second. Just seeing his yard and maybe smelling the air would undoubtedly make him feel better.

All this conflict and fighting was just too much to handle. Bob and Tocho were prisoners in a slave camp, people were dead and dying, Viho was going to blame him, and it was going to get worse before it got better. Who wouldn't walk through the door, given the opportunity? He wasn't a superhero, after all, not even a regular hero. He was a frightened little boy in a man's body, and he was caught in a vicious current.

He shook his head as his hand reached for the doorknob, coming back to reality, and remembered why he was here. Eissa was waiting for him, and the minutes were ticking by. While he was standing here thinking about running away, a man was laying back there dying because of an idea that Quentin had pushed.

He slapped himself across the face, focusing on the sting to drag his thoughts back to the task at hand, and changed the dimension selector back to 107. He activated the door and opened it, not allowing himself to think about anything except getting the torch. He crossed over and raced up to the cabin, berating himself for wasting precious minutes.

The box of tools was on the edge of the porch, right where they had left it. He pulled the torch body out and shoved it in his pocket, and lifted out the small propane cylinder. There were a variety of screwdrivers in the box, and he grabbed a large one. He turned to go back, and remembered that he needed a way to light the torch. A few more long seconds of rummaging through the box, and he found a striker. He ran back to the door, which was still standing open, and crossed back over. He hit the emergency kill switch in the panel, kicked the door closed, and raced back up the path.

Eissa glanced at him as he barreled into the clearing.

"That was quick, you did good. Get the torch fired up, let's get this done."

A massive wave of guilt washed over him. His hands shook as he threaded the torch onto the cylinder and lit it, and he avoided looking at Eissa. He knew she would read his face, and know exactly what he had almost done.

Eissa held the screwdriver tip in the flame, and barked orders at the same time.

"Get that bucket of water over here," she said. "Is it still hot?"

The young woman nodded. "It's warm, but not hot anymore."

"It'll have to do. Start washing his arm. You, keep the pressure on it until I tell you. When I say clear the wound, you pull the packing out of it and get out of the way. You, as soon as she gets the packing out, you wash it fast, I mean in two seconds, and get out of the way. Viho, I need you and two others to hold him still, and two more on his legs. This is going to hurt like you can't imagine. I gave him what pain meds I've got, but it won't help much for this."

The man moaned and raised his head as Viho sat down behind him. Viho placed a strip of leather in the man's mouth for him to bite down on, then wrapped his arms around his chest. When the others were in place, Eissa pulled the screwdriver out of the flame and inspected it. "Okay, is everyone ready?"

They nodded.

"Clear the wound. Wash and go, go."

Eissa stepped over and stuck the tip of the glowing orange screwdriver into the bullet hole. Quentin heard the flesh sizzle for an instant before the man began screaming. His whole body went rigid, and Viho grunted and strained to hold him down. The other four men who were holding his arms and legs struggled equally hard.

The smell hit Quentin totally unexpectedly. It was as if he had just walked into the kitchen at his grandmother's house when he was a kid, and she was frying chicken on the stove. He realized with horror that his stomach was rumbling. He shook himself, and noticed that he was still holding the burning torch. Questioning his sanity, he turned off the fuel supply.

The screams continued for a few more seconds before the man finally passed out. Eissa finished cauterizing the wound. Only Viho watched; the others turned their heads away. The smell hung in the air, and Quentin's stomach rumbled again. Eissa plunged the screwdriver into the ground and wrapped the wound in a dressing.

Quentin turned around, looking for a safe place to set the torch down. The litter crew returned with the DimCorp guards, and he realized that more time had gone by than he thought.

"I've got to go," he called to Eissa. "I don't know if Mazik sent word back to the camp yet or not. Have you got everything under control here?"

"I've got this, go, go." She waved him away, and turned back to the other patient.

Quentin motioned to the Viho and the waiting men. "Alright, let's go."

They jogged down the trail. Quentin was grateful for every morning that Tocho had made him jog up and down the beach in the last month. He was suffering right now, but he probably would have had a heart attack if they hadn't been trying to get in shape. Viho ran silently behind him, never once falling behind.

Mazik met them just before the tree in the trail, and Quentin bent over and placed his hands on his knees, gasping for air.

"Is everything okay here?" he wheezed.

Mazik nodded. "I sent two of the pack carriers back to the camp with the story. We should have about an hour to get ready, maybe a little longer."

"Okay." Quentin stood up and put his hands on his hips. "Does anyone have any water?"

"Come over here, we have water and chocolate." Mazik smiled. "We also have eight extra people to help us guard the guards."

Quentin and Viho followed him around the tree. They had the guards sitting in twos, back to back. Their hands were bound at the wrist, and their upper arms were tied to each other's arms. Another piece of rawhide was tied to each man's throat, with the opposite end tied to the feet of the man behind him. If either of them tried to do anything, it would choke the other one.

"Is Morgan Gage here? Please tell me he's not one of the guards we killed."

"No." Mazik shook his head.

"Okay, so we are down two archers and a litter carrier," Quentin said, returning the canteen and wiping his mouth on his shoulder. "Have you told their replacements where they're going to be, and which target to focus on?"

"Yes, we've been trying to get everyone ready while we waited. We've still got thirty-three archers for the second ambush, so we've got plenty of people." He paused, clearly nervous about saying something.

"Come on, tell me what you need to tell me," Quentin said.

"Some of the men want to know why we aren't using the guns," Mazik said, looking down. He shuffled his feet.

"Have any of them ever fired a gun before?"

Mazik shook his head. Quentin raised his voice so that the rest of the Bribri could hear him.

"Do any of you know how to work a rifle?"

Mazik shook his head again. "No, but it looks easy."

"If you don't know how to eject the magazine and re-load it, or see how many bullets are left, or how to chamber a round and turn off the safety, then you're way better off with the bow and arrow that you're comfortable with. If you only have one second, which was about how long they had this morning, and you pull the trigger and nothing happens, then one of us is going to die." Quentin looked around. "Does that make sense to everyone?"

A few heads nodded.

"In the military, those guys spend months and months learning how to shoot a gun, and how to troubleshoot it if something goes wrong. Months. We have about an hour. Forget it."

"Think on this," Viho added. "This morning, the guards had guns, and you had bows. Who won?"

Quentin watched their eyes light up, and silently thanked Viho for his wisdom. Somehow, Viho had been able to say more in one sentence than Quentin could with five minutes of explanation. Another thing to work on.

"Okay, it's time to get moving. Who's staying to guard

the guards?"

All the Bribri who had been part of the trade convoy raised their hands, as well as four of the archers.

"Okay. Let's move out."

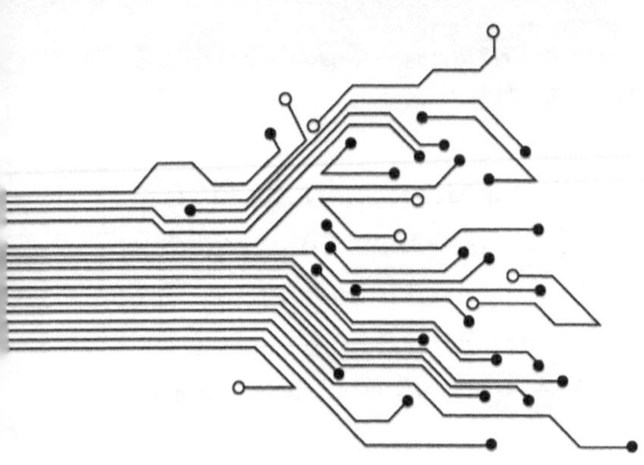

CHAPTER 15

"**I** want you to have some boxes built," Macalister said. "Put the cane processing on hold for the day, this is a new priority. I don't know if those motherfuckers are alone or not, but I ain't taking any chances. We're burying the gold today."

"I don't think we've got enough lumber to crate it up," Gage said. "We may have to pull the walls off of one of the equipment lockers or something to do it."

"I don't care if you have to tear down one of the goddamn shacks back there in shanty town, just make it happen."

"Yes, boss." Gage turned to leave the office, but before he reached the door, it flew open and Bader rushed in.

"I know, boss," Bader said. "I should have knocked, but two slaves from the trade convoy this morning just came back. They said they got attacked by the Cabecar tribe and robbed, and the guards are pinned down out in the woods."

"What?" Macalister was incredulous. He rose halfway out of his chair, a look of confusion and disbelief on his face. "What the fuck are you talking about?"

"The trade convoy got hit, boss," Bader repeated. "They need help. They're pinned down on the side of the trail, trapped."

"Fuck, fucking fuckity fuck-fuck!" Macalister screamed. "What the fuck is happening around here all of a sudden?"

He slammed his hand on the desk, and immediately regretted it. It was still sore from punching Bob yesterday, and it instantly began throbbing again. He covered his face with his hands and took a few breaths, trying to get himself under control. He lowered his hands after a moment and looked at Gage.

"Alright. Take twenty of the guards and go find the convoy. Take one of the slaves that came back as a guide. Maximum goddamn prejudice, Gage, you hear me?"

Gage nodded. "Do you want me to shut down operations here, and put everybody on lockdown?"

"No, they can work without you. Bader will handle it. Go."

Gage left, and Macalister turned to Bader.

"Am I losing my mind, or has the whole world gone batshit crazy all the sudden?"

"Lots of crazy things happening, boss."

"Since when do the Cabecar have the balls to hit one of my goddamn convoys?"

"I don't know boss, that's a new one on me."

Macalister paused, and a smile played at the corners of his mouth. "That's a pretty small tribe, and they're close. If they want to play this game, I'll start hitting them to fill in our work force. Those motherfuckers don't have any idea who they just fucked with."

He rapped his knuckles lightly on the desk and looked out the window. What could have possessed them to rob a convoy? The Cabecar hadn't made a peep in all the years that Macalister and DimCorp had been next door. They even traded chocolate for fish once in a while, if the DimCorp camp was running low on food. Something must have changed, a new leader or something. Or an outsider…

He jumped up and grabbed his hat and whip.

"Come on, we're going to talk to that European fucker that tried to rob us yesterday." He threw the door open and stepped out into the sunshine.

Gage was just marching the rescue team towards the front gate.

"Gage," Macalister shouted across the courtyard.

Gage trotted over. "Yes, boss?"

"If there's a white guy with the Cabecar, I want him alive. If there's more than one, I want as many of them alive as you can bring back. And any Cabecar you can bring back will go to work in the new fields, so try to bring some back. Got it?"

"Got it." Gage jogged back across the courtyard, and Macalister and Bader turned towards the back of the compound.

When they arrived at the equipment locker, there were two guards standing in front of it.

"What the fuck is this?" Macalister asked. "I said four guards at this door at all times."

"Gage just took the other two guys for the rescue detail, boss."

Macalister sighed, knowing that he would have made the same decision that Gage had made. "Open the door."

He stepped inside, and was immediately assaulted by the stench of urine and sweat. Bob and Tocho sat on the box, leaning listlessly against the wall. Bob's eye was purple, and swollen completely shut. His nose was caked with dried blood, and his hair, mustache and beard were filthy and buzzing with flies.

Macalister steeled himself against the foul smell, and fixed Bob with a menacing stare. "I'm going to ask you some questions, and if you lie to me, I'm going to start breaking bones. Is that clear?"

Bob turned his head towards Macalister. His good eye rolled up slowly, and he carefully licked his lips. "Water," he whispered. "Please."

"You tell me what I want to know, you'll get some water. Now, are you two working alone, or are there other people out there from your group?"

"Alone."

"Are you working with the Cabecar people? Do you have some deal going with them?"

"Who?" Bob asked.

"Cabecar. Small tribe, lives north of here on the lake somewhere."

"No, I don't think so."

Macalister made a fist, and then thought better of it. He stepped back, and motioned to Bader.

Bader stepped forward and grabbed Bob by the hair. He snatched Bob's head down to his knees, and at the same time he slammed the point of his elbow into Bob's lower back. Bob let out a hoarse scream, twisting up in agony as he tried to escape a second blow. Bader lifted him up and threw him back against the wall.

"My fucking convoy got attacked this morning," Macalister shouted. "It's pretty fucking hard for me to believe that you don't have something to do with that."

Bob tried to say something, but he couldn't make it out.

"Bring a bucket of water in here," he shouted out the door. "Now."

He turned back to Bob. "I'm going to stick your head in that bucket when it gets in here, and I might be mad enough to just keep it in there and solve this problem right now. You better start talking."

"We've never met the Cabecar," Tocho spoke up. "We only met the Bribri."

"I don't remember asking you a goddamn thing," Macalister turned to Tocho, his eyes blazing. "I don't know where you're from, but around here the jungle monkeys don't say a goddamn thing until I tell them to. Do you understand me? You keep your fucking mouth shut."

The guard brought in a bucket of water, and set it next to Bader.

"Let him have a drink," Macalister said. "Then he won't have any excuses."

Bob leaned forward and plunged his hands into the bucket. He splashed water on his face, and lapped it out of his cupped hands. He got another handful and offered it to Tocho, gasping with pain as he turned.

"He's a goddamned boy scout," Macalister said. "Two inches from death, and he's trying to give his slave a drink."

He stood there staring as Tocho drank from Bob's hands. When he was done, Bob carefully wiped his nose with his wet hand. "Thanks for the water." His voice was raspy, but stronger. "Your guards haven't given us anything."

"Who attacked my convoy? Was someone else with you when you were spying yesterday? Were you gathering information for this attack?"

Bob shrugged and let out a sigh as he looked up at Macalister. "Mr. Macalister, I don't think there's anything I can tell you. If I tell you the truth, which I have, then you don't believe me, and you punish me. If I lie to you, you punish me. Do you see what's happening here?"

Macalister seethed with anger as he realized that Bob was making a valid point. That put him in an impossible position;

if he conceded that Bob was right then that gave Bob power, and that wasn't an option. He decided to stick with his tactic.

"I don't think you've told me the truth yet, not the whole truth."

"I'm sorry that your convoy got attacked," Bob said slowly. He shifted on the box with a wince. "No one is sorrier about that than me. I'll probably be pissing blood the rest of my life over it. But I'm telling you, I have nothing to gain by attacking you. I was trying to set up a long-term trade deal with you, shipping chocolate to Europe. That was always the plan. I don't know what else to say."

Macalister stared hard at him. It was conceivable that the two events happening together were coincidence, but the odds were stacked against it. On the other hand, setting up an export deal to a civilized continent could be a major cash cow. If Bob turned out to be legit, then he could become Macalister's ticket out of here. He could ride a ship to Europe and retire in whatever passed for London or Paris in this dimension when he was ready, rather than trying to go to an unknown dimension on his own. Someone like Bob on the outside would make all of it considerably easier.

He turned to Bader. "Go get these guys some food and another bucket of water so they can get cleaned up."

He took a step towards the door, and turned back. "When my guys get back from rescuing the convoy, we'll see what they found. I hope for your sake that they don't find anyone who knows you. If they don't, then maybe we'll talk about this trade deal."

He walked out without waiting for a response.

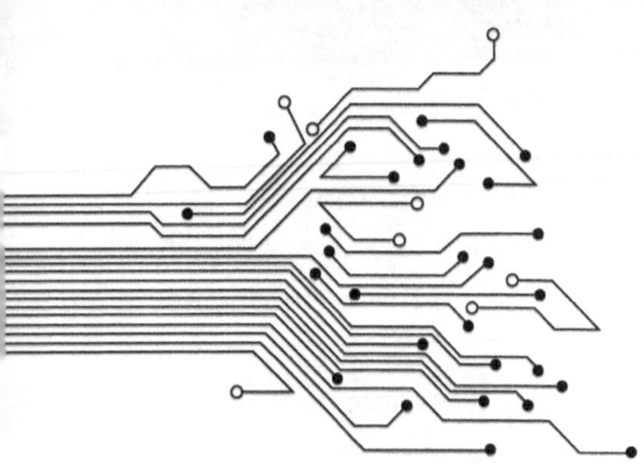

CHAPTER 16

Morgan Gage brought the platoon to a halt outside the gate.

"Jonesy, I want you to set a medium pace. I want to get there quick, but I don't want anybody to be winded. We gotta be ready for whatever's waiting on us."

"Roger that, boss."

"Everybody keep your eyes open, especially you up front. We don't know what the situation is, or what's changed. Round in the chamber, weapons on safe. No accidents. Got it?"

A chorus of affirmative grunts echoed off the wall behind him.

"Alright, let's do this. Jonesy, keep an ear out in case I call a halt. The convoy worker will stay with me and let me know when we're getting close."

They set off down the trail towards the forest at a light jog. Gage tried to think of all the things that might be waiting for them, but the events of the morning were swirling around in his mind, each vying for attention.

He had started his plan yesterday of working on looking sick. That was a hard thing to fake, so he had decided to eat a few handfuls of raw cacao every few hours. Cacao is very rich, and he knew from experience that if he ate too much he would make himself sick. The last time he had overdone it, he had turned pale, vomited, and had intense sweating. If he could reproduce that and maintain it for a day or two, that would certainly get him a pass to the Genesis Dimension to see a doctor.

He hadn't even made it to his third dose of cacao when the field guards had showed up with the two old guys and opened up that whole shit pot. That put him in the position of not feeling good and having to manage a 4-person guard detail, which totally wrecked the duty roster. He still hadn't worked all the bugs out of that this morning, when Macalister had tried to fuck it all up again with his box-building plan.

Gage had been on the verge of telling him he was sick, since Macalister hadn't noticed, when Bader came in with the news about the convoy. That had *really* thrown a wrench in the works. Now he was running through the woods on some crazy rescue mission. He still felt like shit from all the cacao he had forced himself to eat, but now getting across to the Genesis Dimension was all but impossible for the foreseeable future. What an unbelievable clusterfuck this whole thing had turned into.

The shade inside the forest was a welcome relief from the heat of the sun. He was sweating profusely, but it felt cleansing, in a way, and he hoped that by the time they got where they were going, he would be feeling normal again. The rhythmic sound of the boots hitting the ground in cadence was soothing, and he focused on the mission with an effort.

The workers from the trade convoy told them they were attacked by the Cabecar tribe. They wanted the chocolate. Somehow, they had managed to pin down the convoy, but these two guys had gotten away. They had almost no details, other than a location. They didn't know how many Cabecar there were. They didn't know how many injuries or deaths the convoy team had sustained. They didn't know if the guards had any ammo left. The complete lack of information was frustrating, and Macalister's cavalier attitude about it made it even worse. He was so worried about his damn gold that he barely acknowledged the event, as if it were some minor inconvenience that Gage could go deal with on his way to lunch.

That thought brought him full circle, back to the problem of Vincent Macalister, the gold, and the debacle that he was in. He had hoped to be back in the Genesis Dimension at this very moment, sitting in an air-conditioned office in a comfortable chair, having a civilized discussion with a calm, sympathetic human resources professional. Instead, he was jogging through a big clearing in the woods on a mystery mission towards some guy who looked completely out of place here. Wait, what guy?

"Hold up, hold up." Gage came to a stop with the rest of the platoon, staring at the man on the other side of the clearing. He inclined his head towards the worker from the convoy. "Is this the spot?"

The Bribri worker looked around, shifting from one foot to the other. "I'm not sure, boss," he whispered. "I thought it was further down the trail."

The stranger was tall, white, and obviously not a Cabecar. He looked nervous, but he didn't seem surprised that a platoon of armed men had just run up on him, and he wasn't making any moves to leave or step away from the trail. Gage walked up to the front and stopped beside Jonesy.

"Guards, 360 perimeter," he said. "Eyes open. Let's see what this guy's doing."

The platoon formed a rough circle, facing out in a defensive posture. Half of them dropped down to one knee, rifles at the ready. He took a step forward, flipping the safety switch to the "off" position.

"Don't shoot," the man shouted. He raised his hands and turned in a slow circle. "I'm unarmed. Who's in charge here?"

Gage flipped the safety back on and pointed the rifle away from the man. "I am. Who are you?"

"I'm Quentin James. Who are you?"

"Morgan Gage, DimCorp. I need you to step aside. Some of my men have been attacked by a local tribe, and we're on our way to assist."

"That's why I'm here. I'd like to negotiate a truce with you." Quentin dropped his arms and took a step forward. "I've been waiting for you."

Gage kept his face impassive, but his heart skipped a beat. What in the hell was he talking about, negotiating a truce? Was he working with the Cabecar? Gage flashed back to the last thing Macalister had said as they were leaving camp: *If there's a white guy with the Cabecar, I want him alive. If there's more than one, I want as many of them alive as you can bring back.* He licked his lips and tightened his grip on the rifle.

"Who are you negotiating on behalf of? The Cabecar tribe?"

"No, the Cabecar aren't actually involved in any of this. I represent the Bribri people."

"The Bribri?" Gage struggled to make sense of the situation. Did the Bribri attack the trade convoy? Why would they do that? It didn't make any sense.

"Yes, the Bribri. Can I talk to you one-on-one?" Quentin pointed to a dead tree at the edge of the clearing about twenty feet away.

Gage tried to sniff out a trap. This guy seemed wrong for the role he was playing. He definitely didn't act like a soldier, or a military-type diplomat. He wasn't armed, but he had to have an ace in the hole, if he was here bracing the whole platoon. If it was a trap, then they were already in it. Talking was the safest action to take, at least until he could figure out what was going on.

"Keep 'em at the ready, boys, but don't be trigger-happy. Let me see if I can find out what the hell is going on here."

Gage stepped past Jonesy and walked towards the tree line. He went away from the dead tree, just in case it was an ambush. Quentin followed him, and they stopped in the shade. Gage looked him in the eye, searching for some sign of treachery.

"Thanks," Quentin said. "Sometimes it's hard to be candid when you're talking in front of a group." He grinned and wiped his palms on his pants. "I'm nervous enough as it is."

Gage couldn't detect anything other than sincerity. There was nothing about Quentin that seemed right for this situation. He was shy, nervous, and looked like he belonged in a university library, instead of a third-world jungle.

"Who the hell are you?" Gage asked. "What's really going on here?"

"Like I said, I'm Quentin James, and I'm negotiating on behalf of the Bribri tribe. I'm from another dimension, like you, and I'm here to talk to Vincent Macalister and strike a deal with him for improved conditions for the Bribri workforce."

Gage laughed darkly in surprise. "You've clearly never met Vincent Macalister. He doesn't negotiate with anyone."

"That may be true. We'll see."

"Where's my trade convoy? Have you got some kind of mercenary force holding them hostage? Is that your plan for forcing Macalister to negotiate?"

"They're fine. We are holding them, and a few tried to fight it out, but our goal in this whole thing is that no one gets hurt. I don't want anyone to get hurt, not us, not you. We're here to stop people from getting hurt. Does that make sense?"

Gage shook his head. "No, not really. Maybe you can explain it better, because right now, I hear you telling me that you're holding my guys hostage. You don't seem to think we're going to shoot you, so I'm guessing you have a merc team in the trees, and right now you're trying to keep it from getting ugly because you need live hostages to negotiate with Macalister. Is this really about the Bribri, or are you after something else?"

"Whoa, take a breath," Quentin said, raising his hands. "You sort of get it, but you're misunderstanding our intentions. When I say I don't want anyone to get hurt, I really mean it. I'm a humanitarian. My goal is to unite the Bribri tribe and help them attain a decent quality of life in a way that makes sense to both them and DimCorp."

"So, you're going to demand that Macalister let the Bribri go in exchange for getting his guards back?"

"No, no, nothing like that. I know that won't happen. I want him to let the rest of the Bribri tribe come back to the camp."

Stunned, Gage's eyes opened wide, and his mouth moved without making any sound. *This guy must be out of his mind. Or maybe he had misunderstood. Quentin must work for DimCorp, and he was out here to gather the rest of the Bribri tribe up. Somehow, he had gotten that jumbled in his head. It wasn't surprising, given everything else that he was trying* to manage, and the fact that he was suffering from a cacao overdose.

"I think I was confused, Mr. James. I apologize. So, you're with DimCorp? Do you run a slave-capture team, or labor-acquisition, or whatever they're called?"

"No, I don't work for DimCorp. I want to bring the Bribri people together at the DimCorp camp, but I also want Dim-Corp to provide them with proper accommodations. Freedom, housing, solar power, indoor plumbing, food, medicine, dignity, and all that. That's our trade. Labor for quality of life, just like any free enterprise society, really."

Gage shook his head. If this guy was on the level, he was naïve in a way that was going to get him killed. Idealism was great, but it never worked on the people that it needed to work on.

"Look, man, that sounds great, but it's not going to happen. I don't know who you are, but you're going to get killed, along with a bunch of your people and probably a bunch of mine."

"I've been warned that Macalister's going to be tough. Keme said that you were pretty reasonable, though."

"Keme?" Gage was startled by that. "You've talked to Keme?"

"Not directly, but yes."

"The two old guys," Gage said. "There was someone else with them."

Quentin didn't say anything, but Gage could see the truth written on his face. They were definitely in this together, which made a lot of sense.

"Your friends would be quick to tell you what it's like talking to Macalister. They're getting his 5-star treatment right now."

Quentin cringed at that. He was an open book, and Gage was growing more and more sure that this was not a professional group. On the contrary, they seemed to be a ragtag bunch of amateurs.

"Look, this isn't going to happen. I believe that you are well-intentioned, but you're making a fatal error in underestimating Macalister. Let's just release the convoy, you go on your way, and we'll go on our way, and no hard feelings. If you want to keep anyone else from getting hurt, that's how it happens."

This could never work, not in a million years, but if it did, it would solve almost all of Gage's problems. The thought was alluring. It was a pipe dream, but it was a good pipe dream, pleasant to consider. He shook off the fantasy and prepared to turn back to the trail.

"We have an insurance plan," Quentin said. "We're asking nicely, but we're carrying a big stick."

"This? Having us as hostages might be enough to get you an agreement, but as soon as you leave and we come back, he's going to go right back to business as usual. The only thing that will change will be that you give him free slaves." Which he was about to come get anyway, but this guy didn't need to know that.

"We planned for that. If he doesn't hold up his end of the bargain, we will go to the Aztec and the Inka and tell them that Macalister is planning to come steal all their gold and take them as slaves. That's two massive armies that will come wipe DimCorp off the map in this dimension."

Gage stood in silence for a moment. That was a pretty decent insurance plan, but there was still no way Macalister would ever break. He was physically incapable of submitting to someone outside his chain of command, and especially to a skinny nerd with ideas of equality.

"Like I said, I believe you have good intentions, and I appreciate what you're trying to do, on a personal level. However, it's not going to work. Not here, not with Macalister. Maybe in some other dimension with a slightly less Napoleonic tyrant in charge. I wish you the best of luck with that, but I'm going to ask you to end this crusade right here, right now."

"I can't do that," Quentin said. "It's already in motion."

"I'm going to walk back over to my platoon. You can either call off your boys in the woods and take us to our convoy and release them, or we're going to open fire on the jungle and go get them ourselves. Your choice."

"Gage, don't do this. Please don't do this."

The cry in Quentin's voice as he appealed to him was almost more than he could take. If there was some way he could believe that Quentin had any chance of convincing Macalister to accept his deal, he could probably stand aside from his professional duty and let him go. In reality though, that would get Quentin killed, and maybe Gage too, for letting him go. He turned away and started walking back to the trail.

"Alright boys, prone position, battle ready."

The circle of guards dropped to the ground, the clicking of the safety switches ominous in the silence.

"Gage, wait!" Quentin ran up beside him and grabbed his arm. He turned to face him, hardening himself against whatever Quentin had to say.

"Look, you said you believe in what we're doing. If Macalister won't go along with the plan, we can remove him from his position. That would put you in charge, right?"

Gage hesitated. If they removed Macalister from his

position, whatever that meant, he *would* be acting site supervisor, at least for a little while. DimCorp would want to
know what happened to Macalister, though, and Gage would
probably be found guilty of staging a coup or something.
That would end his career before it really even got started,
and he couldn't risk that.

"What do you mean by 'remove'? I can't allow you to
just go in there and kill him."

"We wouldn't do that. You have a DimGate. We would
just take him to New York City in some other dimension
and dump him in front of a homeless shelter or something."

They stared at one another.

"Think about this," Quentin said. "You and the guards
would benefit from this just as much as the Bribri. You're all
slaves under Macalister. If we do this, then everybody wins.
You, the guards, the Bribri, DimCorp, everyone. Macalister
can win too, if he'll listen to reason. Nobody loses."

It was hard logic to refute. Could he justify letting
Quentin James go talk to Macalister? It would prevent a
firefight, at least with the guards under his command out
here, so there was that angle. Macalister wouldn't care about
that, but DimCorp might.

Gage tried to put himself in Macalister's mindset and
imagine the conversation from his perspective.

"He's going to tell you that he can't just requisition
a hundred toilets and sinks, and solar panels, and all that.
DimCorp will never go for it. Hell, I'd have the same problem."

"You've got a DimGate and a pile of gold," Quentin
countered. "You don't need to requisition anything through
DimCorp, just go somewhere else and buy it."

Gage laughed grimly. "He'll never spend that gold on the Bribri. He wouldn't even spend it on us. That's his retirement plan."

"Would you spend it on the Bribri?"

Gage nodded without realizing it and surprised himself by blurting out a response. "Yeah, I would. They're good people. I like to think I'm a good guy, too, but this isn't about any of that for Macalister. It's just about power. He gets off on owning people." He clamped his mouth shut. Why would he say that to a stranger?

"I get that. He's got no self-esteem, so he has to reassure himself that he has value by dominating everyone else. I know the type."

"That's pretty much it." Gage looked down. What if he just sat out here in the jungle with the guards for an hour? What if it was all over when they got back to camp, and Macalister was gone to some other dimension forever? Could he live with that? What if he kept it from happening? Could he live with *that*?

"What would I tell DimCorp? If I'm running the show the next time they come across, they're going to want to know what happened to Macalister. I don't want to end up in the company jail forever."

"Yeah, I've been in your company jail," Quentin said with a grin. "The beds suck. No mattresses."

Gage looked at him in surprise. He might be an amateur, but Gage had to give him some credit for grit. He might not look like much, but he was bucking a mighty big system.

"Damn, Quentin. You've got me boxed in. I don't know what to do."

"Do the right thing. Gather your guys and go sit in the shade and let us do this."

Gage sighed. This definitely wasn't the right way to accomplish his goal of getting Macalister removed, but it was certainly an opportunity to make something happen, and it seemed to have better odds than going through the official channels. Besides, what if they did manage to talk him into something? Anything would be better than the current system, right?

"Alright," he said at last. His stomach was rolling in circles. He consoled himself with the thought that this was the right action for DimCorp, and the right action for the guards, not just the right action for himself. "What do you want us to do?"

"I'd like you to make a pile of all your weapons. The Bribri will guard the weapons, and you guys can sit in the shade until we come back and get you."

"You want me to go tell my guards to turn their weapons over to the Bribri?"

"I guess that will show us both what kind of leadership skills you have."

Gage burst out laughing. "You're full of surprises, Quentin James."

He turned to the guards. "Alright guys, listen up. Clear you weapons so you don't accidently shoot anybody and gather around. We've got a new plan."

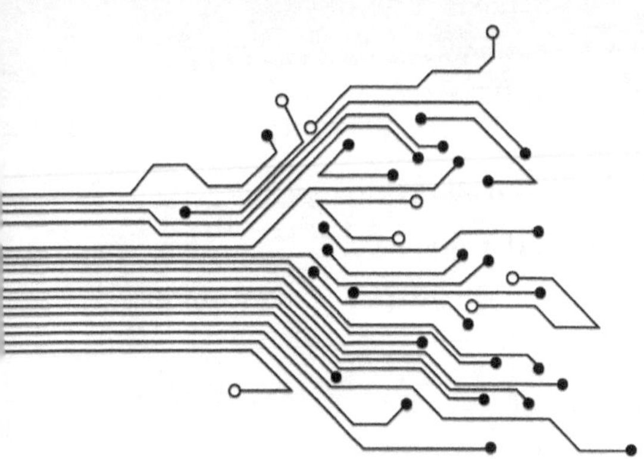

CHAPTER 17

Quentin walked to the dead tree on the other side of the clearing. He was shaking from the incredible adrenaline rush that had washed over him as soon as Gage walked away. He felt like laughing and crying all at the same time. He tried to pull himself together. There would be time for emotions later. Right now, there was still a lot of work to do.

"Viho, Mazik, let's go. We're in business."

Mazik led the restraining crew out of the woods, and Quentin walked over to them. "Change of plans. We're not going to restrain them. Keep at least half the archers in the woods, and the rest of you come sit around the weapons. They are going along with our plan, so let's do our best to keep the peace, okay?"

"Are you sure about that?" Mazik asked. "What if they decide to rush us and take their weapons back?"

"That's why you keep archers in the woods. They've got to stay alert, just in case." Quentin looked down the clearing and nodded at Gage. "He's got a pretty good handle on his men, and he believes in what we're trying to do here, so I think it'll be fine."

Mazik got everyone in place and gave out instructions while Quentin and Viho walked to the side to talk.

"You trust Morgan Gage," Viho said.

Quentin nodded. "I think he realized that we are asking for things that they want too, and don't have."

"He must believe Macalister will give in, or he wouldn't risk crossing him like this."

"No, he's sure that Macalister won't give in. If he doesn't, then we're going to take him through the DimGate to another dimension and leave him there. That will put Gage in charge of the camp."

Viho was silent for a moment before he replied. "That won't be easy. He will still have men there to protect him."

"I think we can manage them. If we announce that Macalister is being relieved of his command, and that Gage is assuming command, we'll probably get most of them to comply. If some of them don't, then we'll have to deal with that. I don't know how else to handle it."

Viho nodded. "We must take our very best warriors in there with us. If we are inside a building, there will be no room for a bow."

"What do you think? You, me, Mazik, and maybe two others, two fighters?"

"I hope that will be enough. There are ten men there. If there are two at the gate, and we tie them up, then there are only eight. Most of them will be out overseeing the work, so there can't be more than two with Macalister."

"Two is worst case scenario," Quentin agreed. "I'm hoping we get him by himself, or with one guard at the most."

Mazik came over and joined them. "I think we are ready."

"Who would you choose as the two best fighters to take with you? Wrestling, or with a knife, not with a bow."

"Tito is the best in the tribe, but he got shot in the

arm." Mazik looked around the clearing. "So, I would choose Lehta and Pallo."

"Get them," Viho said. "Bring a bucket of ties. I will tell you all the plan on the way to the camp."

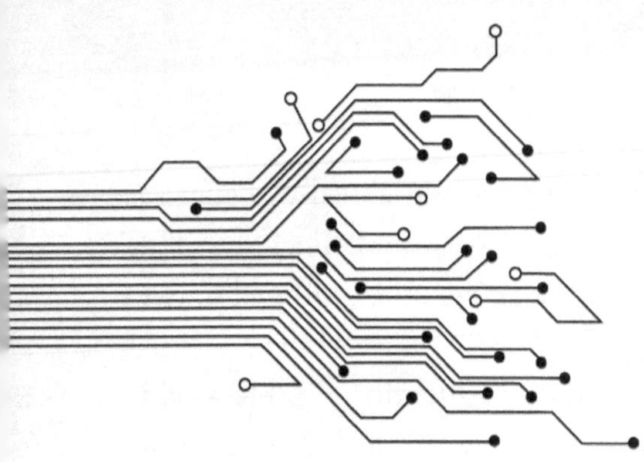

CHAPTER 18

Quentin had to fight off a case of the giggles as they stood at the gate of the DimCorp work camp. The phrase *Take me to your leader* was flashing in the front of his mind like a neon sign. He was dimly aware of the possibility that he might be having a nervous breakdown, or some sort of stress-related break from reality. He reminded himself that he was in the role of an action hero, and maybe a TV lawyer, and action hero lawyers don't giggle.

The lone guard stood on the other side of the barricade, pointing his rifle in their direction, though not directly at anyone. He held his free hand up as they drew near. "Halt. State your name and business."

"Quentin James. We're here to see Vincent Macalister." Quentin looked around, then gestured to his right. "But first, if I could have a private word with you, please?"

The guard stepped to his left, following Quentin's lead and turning his back to the rest of the group. Quentin pointed to the trees to his right, away from the rest of the group.

"Do you see that big dead tree that sort of sticks up above the rest of them? The one with the two branches that kind of look like arms sticking up?"

Mazik materialized behind the guard, snaking his arm around the guard's neck and squeezing the consciousness out of him before he could reply. Quentin grabbed the guard's rifle and kept him from swinging it around. They lowered the guard to the ground quickly, as the others slipped under the barricade.

"Make sure the gag is tight," Quentin said. He stood back as they tied his wrists behind his back. "We need him to stay quiet, even if he wakes up before we get back."

Viho led them across the front of the compound. They stopped at the back of a building, and Viho peered around the corner.

"Okay," he whispered. "We have to get across the open area there, to that house on the other side. There's a guy on the porch sitting in a chair, facing us. That's probably Bader, Macalister's attack dog."

"I think we should just walk over there like we have an appointment," Quentin said. "If we try to act sneaky, we'll just look suspicious."

"Okay." Viho looked over the team. "Is everyone ready?"

Quentin leaned against the wall, pressing his forehead into the wood. His heart was beating wildly, hammering away in his chest as if he had just run ten miles. Until this moment, he hadn't put too much stock in what everyone had to say about Vincent Macalister. Now that it was time to face him, though, he was no longer a mythical creature. He also wasn't some young guard who would be easily bluffed. Quentin had talked a good game about forcing Macalister to see reason. He had almost convinced himself that he could pull this off, even. Almost.

Viho's hand on his shoulder startled him, and he wrenched himself upright.

"Are you okay?"

Quentin sucked in a lungful of air and blew it out. He was miles away from okay, but this wasn't the time to have a heart to heart about self-doubt, especially not with Viho. He forced himself back into character. "Yep. I'm okay. Let's get this done."

Viho nodded. "Do you want me to lead the way?"

"I'll go first," Quentin said. "We'll use the white guy thing again. If I can get him to focus on me, then he won't be focused on you guys. We'll try for the same thing we did at the gate, Mazik."

A strange look crossed Mazik's face, but he didn't say anything. He nodded, his lips pressed into a grim line of determination.

They lined up, and Quentin stepped around the corner and walked towards the man on the porch. His pulse was ringing in his ears, and his heart was dumping adrenaline into his blood at a furious rate. *Act the role, Q. No one knows you. They only know what you show them.* He was halfway across the courtyard when the man looked up and saw him. Quentin squared his shoulders and raised his hand in a friendly wave.

"Hello there," he called out. "We're here to see Mr. Macalister. The guy at the gate pointed us over here. Are we in the right spot?"

Quentin guessed that he had three more steps to reach the porch. He was fully in his role now, the failures of the first ambush and doubts about this meeting pushed aside. He flashed a smile at the stone-faced guard.

The guard stood up and slipped inside the door as Quentin climbed the steps. Quentin ran forward, determined not to lose sight of him.

"Boss, we got company."

The man was opening a door on the right side of the short hall as they came in the front door. Quentin followed him into the room, plastering a big smile on his face.

The man behind the desk swung his feet down to the floor from their perch on the desk and leaned forward, a snarl on his face. "What the fuck—"

"Hi there," Quentin boomed, his deep voice echoing off the mostly-bare walls. "Quentin James, and you must be Vincent Macalister. I hope you don't mind us barging in on you. Is this a good time?"

Vincent Macalister jumped to his feet, and the guard stepped around the desk beside him as they filed into the room and spread out in a half circle. Quentin and Viho stood in front of the desk.

"What's going on?" Macalister demanded. "Who are you? How did you get in here?"

"The gate guard let us in," Quentin said. "Now then, please have a seat. We've got some important stuff to talk about. This is Viho; I believe you two know each other from a long time ago, is that right?"

Macalister's eyes drifted over to Viho for the first time, and an expression of surprise and confusion crossed his face.

"Yes, I can see that you know Viho," Quentin went on. "That's good, it will save us a lot of time explaining things." He grabbed the folding chair and pulled it over. "Please, let's sit down and talk. That's all we're here to do, just talk. Alright?" He gestured at Macalister and sat down.

Macalister sat down slowly, staying on the edge of the seat. He put his elbows on the desk and laced his fingers together, glaring at Quentin. "Alright, we're sitting. Now, who in the hell are you, and what are you doing barging into my office?"

Quentin glanced briefly at Bader before focusing his attention on Macalister. Both men were more physically imposing than he'd expected, and he knew instantly that threatening them physically was out. He was going to have to be smarter than Macalister and maintain his bearing and composure, sticking to his role no matter what.

"My name is Quentin James, as I said. I'm acting as General Counsel for the Bribri people. I represent both halves of the tribe, and we're here to negotiate a settlement with you. If you'll listen to what we have to offer with an open mind, I think you'll find that our terms are not only reasonable, but will significantly benefit both you and DimCorp in the long run, as well as the Bribri people."

Macalister glanced at Viho. "Did you guys form a goddamn union? Is that what this is? You hired some lawyer to come in here and threaten a strike for you?" He leaned back in his chair and relaxed, a smug grin tugging at the corners of his mouth.

"You can think of it as a labor union if you like," Quentin said. "What we would like to do is bring the entire Bribri tribe together in one place. You currently have half the tribe here as slave labor, but what do you think of the idea of having the whole tribe here? Twice the workforce, and more than twice the production."

Macalister's eyes narrowed. "What's the catch?"

Quentin leaned forward in his chair, clasping his hands in front of him. "The catch is that they are free and compensated people, rather than slaves. To be clear, we're not talking about financial compensation, as they aren't interested in money. We want to build decent houses for everyone with running water and solar power, like you've got here. We want good food. We want quality of life items like mattresses and furniture. And lastly, and perhaps most important, we want to transition the guards into a management team that works with the Bribri workforce, rather than dominating them with whips and guns. No more violence. That's the trade."

Macalister steepled his fingers, staring blankly at his desk as he tapped his index fingers together. Quentin marveled at how calm Macalister appeared to be. His own heart was pounding away again, and he was sweating profusely. He consoled himself with the fact that somehow his voice hadn't been shaky while he was talking to Macalister, as he feared it would be.

"How did you think this would work?" Macalister asked, presently. "You think I can just shit building materials? You think I can put in a requisition for a hundred solar panels and no one is going to say anything?"

Quentin smiled, as if there was a joke and they were the only two in on it. "I think you can take some of that gold you've been stockpiling and use your DimGate to go to another dimension and buy what you need."

The smug smile was gone from Macalister's face in an instant, replaced by a mask of rage. "Nope, no fucking way. You can forget about that happening." He shook his head, his jaw clenched.

"Don't be so hasty to say no," Quentin said. "With more people on the workforce, you'll be able to meet DimCorp's production requirements and still keep the chocolate trade going. You'll just have to share the profits with the people who earned them for you, that's all."

"If you think I'm using that gold to buy indoor toilets and bedside lamps for a bunch of fucking cavemen, you've lost your goddamn mind," Macalister said. "And speaking of chocolate, what's your connection to the hit on my trade convoy? Did you hire the Cabecar to attack my men as a distraction?"

"No, nothing like that," Quentin said, straightening back up in the chair. "The Cabecar aren't involved in this at all. Your men are all safe and sound out in the jungle. We'll release them once we've come to an agreement."

"Release them? You captured ten of my guards to use as hostages? Oh, this is too fucking beautiful." He clapped his hands together, and an angry smile exposed his teeth. "I think you'll be in for a surprise when they come trotting back in here any minute." He leaned back in his chair and clasped his hands together behind his head. "Bader, do we have room in the slave quarters? It looks like we've got some volunteers here."

"I assume you're referring to the rescue party you sent out," Quentin said. He was careful to keep his expression and his tone neutral, not taunting like Macalister. "Twenty men, led by Morgan Gage? They're also out in the jungle, waiting patiently."

Macalister's eyes widened, exposing the fear that suddenly gripped him. The color drained out of his face as his hands slid back down to the desk, and it took him a moment to respond.

"Bader, get these fucking assholes out of here, now. I'm not hearing another word of this horseshit."

Bader stepped around the desk, spreading his beefy arms wide as if to sweep them out the door. Pallo was closest to him, and he turned to face Bader.

"Out," Bader shouted, pointing towards the door. With his other hand, he shoved Pallo in the chest. Bader was a head taller than Pallo and strong, clearly stronger than Pallo expected as he stumbled backwards. Bader pulled his pistol out of the holster on his hip. "Get out, now."

Mazik rushed at Bader, and as Bader swung the pistol towards him, he chopped down on Bader's wrist with the edge of his hand. The gun fell to the floor, and Mazik slammed his elbow into Bader's stomach.

The impact rocked Bader, but only slightly. He grabbed Mazik by the forearms and twisted sideways, attempting to throw him to the ground. Mazik surprised him by letting his arms go limp, and as Bader turned, Mazik grabbed the same wrist that he had just chopped with both hands.

Mazik dropped flat on his back and pistoned his legs up, wrapping them around Bader's arm. When his ankles were locked together, he rolled to the right, twisting Bader's arm around. Bader screamed and dropped to the floor, trying to keep his arm from being ripped out of his shoulder socket. As he spun around on the floor, he kicked the pistol, which skittered across the floor and hit Quentin's foot.

With a lightning-fast move, Mazik released his wrist and rolled on top of Bader's back, trying to get a choke hold on him. Bader rolled, throwing elbows back into Mazik's ribs as he rolled on top of him.

Quentin shook himself. The sudden onslaught of violence had caught him by surprise. He tried to determine the best way of getting the situation back under control as he stood up.

Suddenly, Bader produced a knife. He slashed at Mazik's legs, as Mazik fought to get his forearm back across Bader's throat. Bader rolled again, and swung the knife over his shoulder at Mazik's face. Mazik released the choke and grabbed Bader's hand with both of his, using the momentum of the swinging arm as he forced the knife down and into the base of Bader's neck. Bader went rigid, his legs spasming as blood poured down his chest. He slowly slumped forward.

"Enough," Quentin shouted. "This stops right now. Someone help Mazik get his leg wrapped up." He turned back to Macalister. "This is what I mean, this has to stop-"

Macalister had his hand in his desk drawer. The words died on his lips as he watched Macalister stand up, pulling a gun out of the drawer. He pointed the gun at Mazik.

"No," Quentin screamed. "Don't do it!"

Macalister turned towards Quentin, first with his eyes, and then with his body, swinging the pistol around to bear on him. The movement seemed to take forever, yet Quentin stood frozen in place, unable to think, much less act. The flash of fire from Macalister's gun surprised him, but nowhere near as much as the impact of the slug to his chest.

It felt like someone hit him with a sledgehammer, and he fell back into the chair, the wind knocked out of him. He tried to inhale, but the air couldn't get past his throat. Another slug hit him, and he looked down as his ribs screamed in protest of the beating. He tried to breathe again, again with little success. The third attempt managed to get some air into his lungs, which quelled the rising panic. The pain was excruciating, but the renewed flow of oxygen made it bearable.

Bader's pistol lay on the floor in front of him. It was a symbol of everything they were here to fight against: violence, tyranny, and oppression. On the other hand, it was also a symbol of hope, a way to end the violence before anyone else got hurt. Quentin was torn. The vest had saved his life, but no one else had such a luxury. If he allowed Macalister to shoot someone else, it would be the same as if he had shot them himself. If he managed to pick up the gun and shoot Macalister, though, he would carry that on his conscience forever. It would take a team of therapists to make him functional again. Granted, if Macalister killed someone else, he would need therapy to deal with the guilt from that, too. It was a lose-lose situation, and Macalister's unwillingness to listen to reason was infuriating. He couldn't just sit there, he had to do something. Macalister had to be stopped, since there was clearly no reasoning with him.

If I could just grab the gun, he thought. *I don't think I can bend over, but I need that gun.* Instantly, the gun flew up and into his hands. He stared at it, puzzled for a moment. Was he dreaming? Then it occurred to him: the micro movers.

He looked up. Macalister was staring at him in shock, with his gun still pointed at the floor in front of Quentin. Quentin lifted the pistol, amazed at how heavy it was, and pointed it at Macalister. He cocked the hammer with his thumb, hoping there wasn't a safety on it. His ribs were screaming in pain, and it was all he could do to keep his arms extended. Macalister's eyes narrowed, and he raised the barrel of his pistol back up with a snarl.

Quentin squeezed the trigger, screaming in frustration and pain. He continued to scream as he pulled the trigger again and again, hearing nothing but the deafening thunder of gunfire, and then the sudden silence that followed it. Macalister disappeared in the cloud of smoke. He realized that he was still pulling the trigger as Viho put a hand on his back and gently took the gun out of his hands.

"Quentin, you are shot."

Quentin shook his head and coughed. A bright flash of pain accompanied the cough, and he grimaced. "I'm- I'm okay. I just need a minute."

Viho came around in front of Quentin, staring at him. "I don't understand. How are you not dead? I don't even see blood. And how did you get the gun so fast?"

Acrid smoke hung down from the ceiling, burning Quentin's nose and eyes. He waved his hand, trying to clear it away. He leaned heavily into the chair, as if the weight of the moment were crushing him into it. His chest was throbbing, but his breath was coming easier. He couldn't tell if he was bleeding or not, but the vest appeared to have done its job, at least, so far.

He looked slowly up at Viho and lifted his shirt. "I have a vest. I think it stopped the bullets. Is anyone else hurt besides Mazik?" He looked around, trying to assess the situation.

Viho turned away. "Mazik, are you okay? Do we need to get you back to Eissa so she can stitch you up?"

Mazik was silent, and Quentin looked closer at him. He was sitting beside Bader's body, staring at it as Pallo cut his shirt into strips and tied them over the slices on Mazik's legs. Viho put his hand on Quentin's shoulder.

"That is the man that killed Mazik's father, my oldest son. He is the man that gave Mazik his scar. And now Mazik has killed him."

"Oh, man," Quentin said. "We're going to need to get him some counseling. I'm going to need it too, maybe we can get a group rate or something." He let out a shaky sigh.

"There are still eight guards here," Viho said. "They must have heard the gunfire."

"Oh shit, I forgot all about them. We need to get Morgan Gage here to help us." Quentin climbed wearily to his feet and limped to the window. "I don't see anybody out here. Pallo, can you run back there and get him? Maybe we should stay holed up here until you get back."

"Okay." Pallo finished patching Mazik's leg and headed for the door.

"Get the stretcher crews, too," Quentin called. "We may need to haul Bob and Tocho back, who knows what kind of shape they're in."

His left arm was burning, and he looked down. There was a rip in his shirt sleeve, and a stripe of raw flesh underneath it. He stared at it dumbly for a moment, then looked over at Macalister's body.

Macalister sat in his chair, his head tilted back and his blank eyes staring at the ceiling. His chest was a sodden mass of blood. His gun lay beside him on the floor, and near it were the shell casings, glinting in the light from the window.

Looking at Macalister made him queasy in a way that he wasn't prepared to deal with, so he turned back to the window and watched Pallo make his way across the courtyard towards the front gate.

No one approached the office, and after ten minutes, Quentin decided that in the absence of all their leadership, they probably weren't going to. He turned away from the window. Mazik still sat beside Bader. Viho was sitting beside him with a hand on his back. They were both crying.

There was no way for Quentin to relate to their pain. This was the closing moment on a five-year-old wound, and a moment of justice for their lost family member. There was also the trauma of having killed someone that Mazik had to deal with, and Quentin realized with a start that *that* was something he *could* relate to.

He hadn't really processed the fact that he had shot Vincent Macalister and killed him. He looked over at the body, and the pool of blood on the floor around it. There was already a fly on Macalister's face. He sensed that there was a wrecking ball of reality sweeping towards him, but it hadn't arrived yet. He was still in shock.

"Lehta," he whispered.

Lehta stood near the door, ready for anything. He looked over at Quentin.

"Can you go look around the place and find a sheet or something that we can use to cover up these bodies?"

Lehta nodded, and slipped out the door. He returned a few minutes later with a couple of thin blankets. Together, they covered Macalister; each at an awkward angle as they tried to avoid stepping in the blood.

"Thanks, man. I'm already going to have nightmares about this; I sure don't need to sit here and stare at him."

"You saved Mazik's life. Maybe everyone's life. You did the right thing." Lehta stepped over to Quentin and gripped his forearm. "Thank you, my friend. You are welcome in my home."

Quentin returned the grip, feeling a flood of gratitude sweep over him. "Thank you for saying that." His throat seized up, and he turned away as a rush of tears filled his eyes. It only lasted a moment, but he was tremendously relieved when it was over. His chest even managed to relax slightly. "You are welcome in my home, too. Well, you know, if I had one, you would be." He could tell it was getting awkward, and clamped his mouth shut.

Quentin turned to see Mazik climbing to his feet. He winced as he put pressure on his wounded leg, and hobbled

over to Quentin, leaning on the desk for support. He surprised Quentin by wrapping him up in a fierce hug. The
pressure on his bruised ribs hurt like hell, but he ignored it.
Mazik stepped back after a moment, his face shiny.

"You have given me many things today. You gave me
freedom for my people. You gave me courage by your brav-
ery. You gave me my life when Macalister tried to take it. I
cannot repay you for these things, but you are my brother for
life, and you will always be welcome in my home."

Quentin was at a total loss for words. He certainly
didn't feel like the kind of guy who had done those things.
In contrast, he felt wretched, as if he had done something
terribly wrong that couldn't be undone.

"You're forgetting all the things that went wrong today.
People died because of me, and that's the most awful thing
that could happen. I came here to try to stop bad things
from happening, and instead I made it worse."

Viho clapped his hands once, and they turned to him.

"When I was young, my grandfather told me that one
day I would become the chief of the Bribri people. He told
me that a great leader does two things well: first, they know
the moral code of their people, and second, they know how
to handle people who act outside that moral code. He said
that sometimes you have to step away from the first one to
accomplish the second one, but never to do that unless there
was no other choice."

He looked up at Quentin, and spread his arms.

"There was no other choice. When you are alone at
night with your thoughts, remind them that there was no
other choice. You did the only thing you could do."

Quentin nodded, not trusting his voice. He backed up

against the wall and slid down to the floor, hugging his knees and embracing the throbbing heat in his chest.

Lehta covered Bader's body with the second blanket, then moved over to the window and looked around the camp as the room fell quiet. Quentin wished he had something to relieve the stinging in his arm. Eissa had the cream that had done the trick on his burned wrists, once he got back out there. That caused him to wonder how Eissa was doing with the wounded Bribri. The man she had cauterized came to mind, and he felt guilty for even acknowledging the pain in his arm and chest. That guy could complain about pain. This was nothing.

He jumped when Lehta spoke, realizing that he had zoned out.

"Gage is here."

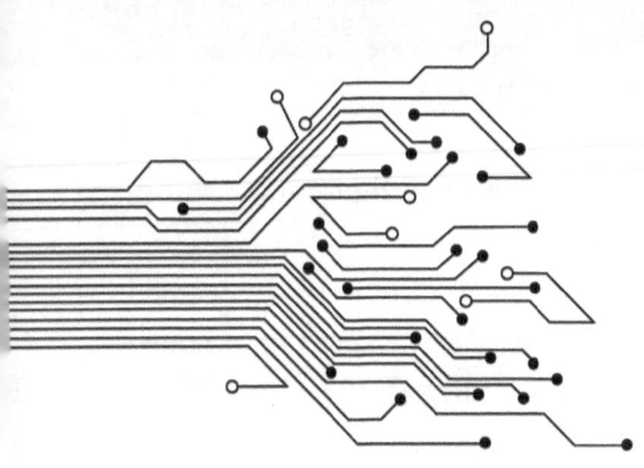

CHAPTER 19

They got to their feet, and Quentin quickly coached himself back into his role. The worst was over, but he still had a lot to do before this would be finished. He moved out to the front porch to meet Morgan Gage. The development of this relationship was more critical now than ever.

"I heard it didn't go very well." Gage paused at the edge of the porch and put a foot up on the step, resting his elbow on his knee.

"No, it didn't go very well at all. Did Pallo tell you that Macalister and Bader are dead?"

"Yeah, he told me."

Quentin looked down, shaking his head. "That wasn't how I wanted it to go."

"That's the only way it could have gone, really. The only thing that was an unknown was who would be standing when it was over."

"I need to find Bob and Tocho. I'm guessing there's a guard wherever they are, so I waited for you so that no one else gets hurt." He was putting it all on the line here. This would be the telling moment on where Gage stood. "Can you help me out with that? Are we still okay?"

Gage looked around the camp, then back at Quentin. "Yes, I think we're still okay. Let's go get your friends, then we gotta sit down and make some plans and figure some things out."

Quentin breathed an inward sigh of relief. Gage seemed to be handling the situation better that he could have hoped for. "Should we go with you, or wait here?"

"You can come with me. You're okay with me here."

He set off walking down the side of the warehouse. Quentin waved at Lehta in the window of Macalister's office, gesturing for them to follow, and stepped down off the porch.

They rounded the corner at the back of the processing building, and Gage gestured to the lone guard at the door. "Open up, Dobson. It's over."

The guard unlocked the padlock and pulled the chain out, stepping to one side. "What's going on, boss? I heard shots fired in the camp, but no one's been back here."

"We'll have a meeting shortly and brief everyone, just hang tight." Gage turned and motioned Quentin forward. "They're going to look a little rough, so brace yourself. Keep in mind that this was all Macalister and Bader."

As the door opened, sunlight streamed into the dark room, illuminating a figure seated on one side. Quentin's breath caught in his throat as he vaguely recognized Bob. His long white hair and bushy white beard identified him, but his face was swollen and purple, almost black in places. His beard was streaked with dried blood. He turned his head and raised a hand to shield his good eye from the sudden light.

"Oh my God," Quentin said. "Bob, it's me, Quentin. How bad are you hurt? Can you talk? Is Tocho in there, too?"

"Easy kid, one question at a time." Bob's chuckle turned into a rasping cough. "We're okay, just a little frayed around the edges."

Tocho leaned forward into the light. "I'm doing much better than Bob. He always gets all the attention. It's because he has a big mouth."

"Come on, let's get you out of there," Quentin said. "There's some guys coming with litters, and we'll get you out to the triage center so Eissa can take a look at you."

"I've had my ass kicked worse than this and walked away from it," Bob said. He attempted to stand up, rolling to his side to avoid using his lower back. Tocho stood up and grabbed him by the armpits, lifting him up. "I might need a little help getting upright, but once I'm there, I ought to be okay."

"Yes, but you were ten years younger the last time that happened," Tocho pointed out. "You'll be grateful for the ride by the time they get here."

"Yeah, yeah." Bob took a shuffling step towards the door, and Quentin moved forward to help him down the step.

"Where have you been, anyway?" Tocho asked. "We beat you here by two or three days."

"We must have taken a wrong turn in Albuquerque," Quentin said with a grin. The fact that Bob and Tocho were alive and standing in front of him was a miracle. That they felt well enough to make jokes, despite the way they looked and felt, was almost enough to make him cry.

"I guess you talked Macalister into your idea, huh? I'm impressed, I don't mind saying. I kind of thought he'd be here to trip me down the stairs." Bob grabbed Quentin's shoulder and eased himself down the step with a grimace. "His flunky really did a number on my back."

"He did a number on your face, too. You look like shit." Quentin turned to Gage. "Is there someplace we can get these guys a shower and some clean clothes?"

"Macalister's house. They can get cleaned up while we talk." Gage turned to the guard. "Gather everyone up at the square; all the Bribri, all the guards. We've got to have that meeting right now."

The guard took off towards the fields, and they began walking slowly back up the side of the warehouse. Bob held on to Quentin's arm as they went, and Tocho stayed on his other side. Viho and Mazik followed behind with Lehta and Gage.

Quentin tried to come up with the right words to tell them what happened with Macalister and Bader. Bob expected people to get killed, and he had warned him over and over that it was probably going to happen, so he wasn't going to be surprised about it. So, what was the problem in telling them that people were dead and wounded?

Ego. Quentin almost smacked himself in the forehead. Of course, his pride wanted to be able to prove to Bob that it could be done with diplomacy instead of violence. He was looking at the situation as a defeat instead of a win because of his ego. He shook his head, grinning at his own idiocy.

"Well, through a delicate balance of violence and diplomacy, we have achieved the first steps toward freedom and gainful employment for the Bribri," he said. He glanced over his shoulder at Viho before continuing. "Vincent Macalister and Bader were casualties of their own cause, as well as three DimCorp guards out on the trail. We lost a Bribri man, too. I'm embarrassed that I don't know his name."

"Wahdondah," Viho said from behind them. "His name is Wahdondah. He made our fish traps. He could make anything."

Bob limped in silence for a few steps. "And Eissa?"

"She's running a triage center out in the jungle," Quentin said. "There were several injuries when we met the trade convoy, as well as the deaths."

Bob grunted. They were nearing the end of the warehouse. "We'll have plenty of time to talk this out. For right now, help me get up these steps. I feel like I've been rode hard, and put up wet."

"Me, too," Tocho said. "I'm so stiff I can't hardly move. I'm upgrading the bed situation at the cabin as soon as we get back. Two nights on a box helped me decide that."

Once Bob and Tocho were settled in at the shower area, Quentin and Gage went back down the hall and opened the door to Macalister's office. The bodies lay where they had left them, and Quentin stopped in the doorway.

"We covered them up. I couldn't keep looking at Macalister."

"Is this the first time you've killed someone?" Gage asked.

"Yes. And hopefully the last."

Gage lifted the blanket and looked underneath. He moved sideways to allow a path for light from the window, and whistled under his breath.

"Damn, you really gave it to him, huh?"

Quentin was uncomfortable thinking about it. "I guess so." The expression on Macalister's face as he swung the pistol towards Quentin was burned into his brain, guaranteed to resurface over and over. The curled lip, the hate-filled eyes that changed to shock and disbelief as the first bullet hit him in the chest, the pain that followed that, it was all there.

"Don't beat yourself up about it," Gage said. "He's hurt a lot of people in his life. A lot of it was verbal abuse, psychological trauma, but I think that's worse than physical pain for a lot of people. Every world is better off without him being in it."

"I'm not cut out to play God," Quentin said. "I really feel horrible about it."

"That'll back off with time. Right now, it's all too fresh to be logical about it. You just gotta ride it out." He let the blanket fall back in place, and turned to Bader's body on the floor. "Now this guy, here's somebody that needed to be killed, if anybody ever did. He's a heartless, sadistic bastard that gets off on hurting people. He did most of the work on Bob, you know."

"Well, that makes me feel a little better," Quentin said.

"Let's go outside and get some fresh air," Gage said. "I'll get some guys to bury these two down by the river somewhere."

Quentin let out a giggle before he could stop himself. Gage glanced at him with his eyebrows raised.

"Sorry," Quentin said. "I was just thinking about a dimension we went to by accident once that still had dinosaurs running around. We could take them there, and really mess with the archeologists that find them a few thousand years down the road."

Gage laughed. "Well, screwing up the historical record would be right up his alley, so there's that."

They made their way out to the porch and sat down on a bench. A few birds were chirping, but it was otherwise quiet.

"Well, let's see," Gage said. "I guess the first thing I need to do is figure out what to tell the crew. I gotta get the rest of them back here pretty quick, so they don't panic and do something stupid."

"Yeah, you need them all to be on board with this. That might be hard with the trade convoy crew, since some of them got killed this morning." Quentin suddenly remembered that they were still tied up. "The first group is restrained, so we need to get out there and release them."

Gage stood up. "You're right, they're going to be pissed. Where are they?"

"Maybe another mile down the trail from where we met you, maybe a little less. The dead are at our triage center. Let's talk to the ones that are here first, though. That way they aren't standing up here wondering what to do with Viho and Mazik while we're gone."

"Yeah, you're right. One thing at a time."

"So, no one knows that Macalister and Bader are dead except for you and us. You need to decide what you're going to tell your guys about that."

Gage debated for a moment. "I think we tell them the truth. No one will be surprised about it, and I don't think too many of them will be very torn up about it."

"Okay. That makes burying them a little easier. Now then, over the next few days- "

"That's the part I'm worried about. I don't even know where to start."

Quentin pulled his notebook out of his pocket, wincing at his protesting ribs. He had a list of things from his brainstorming session a few days earlier that would be necessary for getting things moving, although at that time he thought he would be dealing with Macalister. There was a bullet hole through the edge of it, and he looked at it in wonder, smiling unconsciously. His notes were missing a few letters, but he was able to read around it. "I recommend that you form a committee. Pick a team leader or two from your guys who are smart and dependable, and probably Viho and Keme. It would be a good idea to ask Tahki Ana, too. Sit down and start planning and making lists. Figure out what all you want to do, what you're going to need to do it, and in what order. That will get you started, and it will give you team support from both sides."

"That's smart," Gage said.

Quentin shifted sideways to face Gage. "It's going to take a lot of time to put this together. The Bribri village out there can't move here until you have a place for them to live. Don't try to put everyone to work in the fields tomorrow. You need a planning team, a shopping team that gets materials together from somewhere, a construction team, and so on."

"I've got a couple of guys who are really experienced builders. They'll be a major asset in figuring that stuff out."

"Perfect," Quentin said. "And you need to expect to have some conflict. This is going to be a hard transition for people on both sides. You need to have a lot of training sessions, like ten minutes before every meal, where you talk about conflict resolution. Don't hide it, put it out in front. This is going to be a huge culture change for everyone, and it's going to have plenty of challenges. It'll be worth it, but you might have to remind them of that now and then."

Gage nodded. A line of Bribri men came around the corner on the far side of the warehouse near the mess hall. Gage stood and stepped down into the dirt.

"Everyone gather around," he called out. "We'll wait until everyone gets here."

Quentin turned as the door beside him opened. Viho stepped out on to the porch, and suddenly ran out into the courtyard.

"Keme!" Viho shouted. "Keme!"

Quentin watched as a man stepped out of the group of Bribri and raced towards Viho. They crashed together in a bear hug, shuffling in a circle as they tried to keep from falling. At last, they managed to pull apart.

"You look terrible," Keme said. "You look like an old man. I guess I probably do, too."

Viho laughed. "You look-" He trailed off, running his fingertips across the scars that covered Keme's chest and shoulders. "This will not happen again. You look like a free man."

Keme's face lit up with a smile. "I earned every scar," he said, his voice filled with pride. He pointed to a jagged scar on his right arm. "For that one, a boy who dropped a jar of cane juice didn't have to get beaten. This one got my team a water break when it wasn't break time. This one I got for telling Macalister that he hurts himself more than he hurts me."

Viho hung his head for a moment. When he looked back up at Keme, there were tears running down his cheeks. "You are a true leader. I would not have been as great as you if I had stayed here instead. I'm so sorry that you carried this load, but for the Bribri, I am grateful that you did. I am shamed for my weakness."

Keme pulled Viho back into his chest and hugged him tightly. "You are a great leader, don't think that you aren't. Our people on the outside have lived a quiet, peaceful life. I could not have given them that; I would have killed them all trying to fight DimCorp. You are the wise one, my brother."

Quentin's eyes filled with tears as he watched them. The more he learned about them, the more complex everything became. Had he thought about the sacrifice that these brothers had made every day for the last five years? It didn't seem like he had any understanding of what had really been going on here until now. Maybe it was better that way.

Gage grabbed Bader's chair off the porch, carried it out into the courtyard, and stood up on it.

"Alright, do we have everyone? How many guards are here?"

Quentin realized that the guard at the front gate was still tied up. "There's one more," he said, running across the square. "I'll go grab him."

By the time he returned with the groggy guard, Gage had everyone gathered around him. Quentin stopped at the back of the crowd and listened.

"This is a new day. Starting today, there are new rules, new ideas, a new life, and a new leader."

He looked around the crowd, making eye contact with some of them.

"Vincent Macalister is dead. Paul Bader is dead. The way they did things around here is dead."

One of the guards cheered. It echoed off the back of the warehouse in the silence, and suddenly the whole crowd erupted in cheers. Gage gave them a moment to get it out.

"Viho and Keme are going to help me turn this place into a town that we are all happy to live in," he continued. "No more slavery. From now on, we all work together. We all benefit from our efforts. We will live like civilized people. We will all have dignity."

The crowd cheered again. Quentin looked around, trying to gauge the reaction of the guards. Most of them looked stunned, but they were all grinning and whispering to each other.

"I need you to be patient with me, and patient with one another as we figure out how to do this. It's going to take time, and it's going to take a lot of hard work. Right now, I've got to go get the rest of the guards. I need some volunteers to help me get some things done. The rest of you, take an early lunch while we figure out what to do next."

He stepped down off the chair. Quentin drifted around the edge of the crowd and made his way back to the porch. He glanced inside the door, where Tocho was coming down the hall.

Quentin stepped inside the hallway. "How's Bob?"

"His spirit is indestructible. His body, on the other hand, is going to need some time to recover."

"Do you think he can get back to the DimGate so we can get him to the cabin? We've got some people coming with a litter, so we can carry him if we need to."

Tocho nodded. "That will probably be best. I don't think he could walk that far right now, but he could ride."

"Okay, we'll do it that way. I'd like to get out of here as fast as we can, so as soon as you guys are ready, we'll head out."

Quentin went outside to find the litter crew, leaving Tocho to get Bob ready to go. Gage waved him over from the edge of the courtyard, where he was talking with a group of guards.

"What's up?" Quentin asked.

"I'm ready to go get the rest of the crew when you are. I think we both need to be there, so nobody gets hurt."

"Agreed. I'm just trying to find the litter crew so we can carry Bob back with us. We'll meet you at the front gate in ten minutes."

By the time Quentin got back to the house, Tocho and Bob were waiting on the porch. Bob looked a little better with the blood and mud washed out of his hair and beard, but his face was still swollen and discolored.

"You look like hell," Quentin said with a grin.

"I feel like hell," Bob said. "But that's a significant improvement over how I felt an hour ago."

"We'll get you out to Eissa, and she'll have you feeling better in no time."

Once Bob was situated in the litter, Quentin led them to the gate, where they met up with Gage and two of his men.

"Okay," Quentin said. "Is everyone ready?"

Gage nodded. "Lead the way."

Quentin set off at a light jog, and the others filed in behind him. It was quiet in the jungle, other than the sound of footsteps and breathing, and the man softly calling cadence for the litter carriers. Quentin's chest was feeling better, and the exercise warmed and relaxed his sore muscles. The only time anyone spoke was when they stopped to trade out litter carriers.

On the second stop, Gage walked back to the litter. "I'll take a turn," he volunteered. "I'm pretty tall though, so I need someone over six feet to partner with."

"I'll try it out," Quentin said. "I don't know if my chest can handle it, but we'll see." He looked down at Bob. "Are you hanging in there?"

Bob nodded. "I feel guilty as hell riding in this thing, that's all. What's wrong with your chest?"

"Oh, Macalister shot me a couple of times. Nothing serious." Quentin tried to look smug as he hefted his corner of the litter, and made some experimental motions. It wasn't bad, surprisingly. That was a good indication that he didn't have any broken ribs, just bruising. "I think I'm good. If that changes, I'll let you know."

Gage glanced over at him, surprised. "Are you wearing a vest or something?"

Quentin nodded. "It seemed like the prudent thing to do, although I thought I might get shot out here on the trail, not in the office. That came as a surprise."

They set out again. Two Bribri men carried the front of the litter, and Quentin and Gage carried the rear end. The heat was building in the jungle as the morning crept towards afternoon, and Quentin was sweating freely. Gage ran beside him, showing no signs of fatigue despite having just made the run in to the camp from out here. Quentin focused on matching Gage's stride, and before he knew it, they were coming into the first clearing.

They paused in the middle of the trail, in between the group of DimCorp guards and the Bribri.

"DimCorp, listen up," Gage called. "I'm going to go get the trade convoy, and then we'll come back here. We'll go over everything once we've got everybody together, and then we'll head back to camp. Roger that?"

"Roger that, boss."

"Okay. Just so everybody knows, as of right now the Bribri are no longer slaves. They are free men, and we're all going to be working together as a team." Gage looked closely at his men. "There's not going to be any trouble. No fighting, no attitudes. Roger that?"

"Roger that." They answered together in unison, although some of them looked at each other in surprise.

They traded positions on the litter, and Quentin led them out the other end of the clearing. His shoulder felt light after carrying the litter, and he flexed his fingers as well as his arm, which felt like it had been stretched at least a foot. His chest was aching, but his quick recovery so far gave him a whole new appreciation for the vest's ability to protect him. He made a mental note to send Jake a fruit basket or something the next time they were in Dimension 443.

He slowed them down to a walk as they approached the second clearing.

"Hello, the Bribri," he called out, holding up his hand to stop the line behind him.

He listened for the answering call, and carefully walked into the clearing once it came. Everyone sat where they had left them, bound back to back.

"Okay, listen up," Quentin said. "We are going to release you now. Morgan Gage is here, and he's going to brief you on the situation. Bribri, you all come with me once we release the DimCorp guards."

"Quentin, what's the plan from here?" Gage asked. "For you and me, I mean. Do you want to schedule a meeting in a day or two, or how do you want to proceed?"

"For right now, I'm going to leave it to you and Viho and Keme. I need to get Bob some medical attention." He stuck his hand out to Gage. "You don't need me, anyway. You know what needs to be done better than I do. I'll check back in with you in a few days."

Gage grinned and shook his hand. "I don't even know what to say to you. You came in here and turned the whole world upside down in a day."

Quentin flushed. "Lots of people made this happen. I just wish that we could have done it without losing anyone."

"Well, most people wouldn't have even tried to do it peacefully, so I commend you for doing what you did. And like I said, sometimes the world is better off without certain people in it."

He clapped Quentin on the shoulder with his other hand,

then released him and stepped back. "You better get going."

When the guards had been released, Quentin led the Bribri out of the clearing and towards the triage center. Tocho moved up the line and walked beside him.

"I'm glad you're walking now. I don't think I can run anymore."

Quentin laughed. "You're pretty spry. I think you could probably outlast everyone here."

"I was watching you and Morgan Gage. He respects you. You must have handled this whole thing very well."

Quentin felt his face grow warm and fumbled for something to say in response. "I tried to do what I thought you and Bob would do," he finally managed.

"Bob and I probably would have blown up the mess hall while they were all eating dinner," Tocho said. "I don't know how well this went, but it seems like you managed to not make a war out of it."

"Lots of people died," Quentin said. "I think it was five people from DimCorp, and a Bribri man. We also had a couple of Bribri men injured with bullet wounds. It seems to me like it turned into a war."

Tocho glanced at him. "I understand what you're feeling, but you need to put logic and feelings together. They're both important parts of this. Logically, this mission was a success. The goal was met. It hurts that there were people lost, but that doesn't make it a failure. Can you see that?"

Quentin nodded. "I see your point. It's going to take a while for my stomach to agree, though."

Tocho smiled, and clapped him on the back. "By the way, thanks for getting us out of there. I forgot to say that earlier."

Quentin slung his arm around Tocho's shoulders, and hugged him as they walked.

"I owed you a rescue," he said. "You all got me out of DimCorp's jail. Besides, you're the only one who knows where everything is buried."

They both laughed, and Quentin felt better than he had in days. They walked on in a comfortable silence.

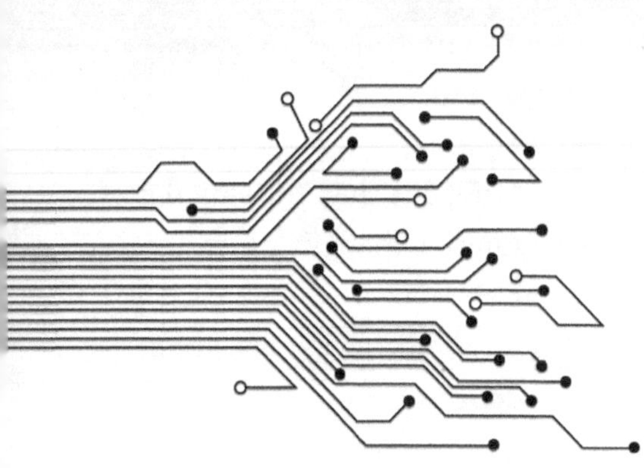

CHAPTER 20

Eissa handed the bag of fluids to Quentin. "You're going to have to hold this, since we don't have any I.V. hangers here."

"I could probably use some fluids myself," Quentin said, moving around beside Bob. "I ran about three marathons or so today."

Eissa barely glanced at him. "Drink some water."

"Carrying me on a stretcher, I might add," Bob said. "That's no easy feat."

"Hierarchy of needs," Eissa said. "Injuries first. He'll manage."

She checked the drip rate on Bob's fluids, then glanced over at Tocho's. She grabbed the wrist of the woman who was holding Tocho's fluids, and raised it up. "Hold it right here, no lower."

The woman nodded, and Eissa walked over to check on her other patients. The man she had cauterized was awake, and they watched as she checked his vitals and noted them on her clipboard.

"She's totally in her element," Bob said. "I've never seen her so engaged. She was smiling while she sewed up Mazik's leg."

"I think she definitely performs better when everything is falling apart around her," Quentin said. "She needs counseling to get through normal life, but she's thriving out here. You should have seen her cauterize that guy's arm."

"If you recall, we had a conversation a while back on the beach," Tocho said. "We talked about having a sense of purpose. I think this is her purpose."

She finished her rounds, and came back over to them. "So, how did it go at the camp? Did Macalister agree to the deal?"

Quentin's stomach lurched, and his mouth filled with saliva. For a moment he thought he was going to vomit, but it passed quickly.

"Your face just went pale," Eissa said. "Are you all right?"

"Yeah, I'm okay." Quentin wiped the cold sweat off his forehead with his free arm. "I just, well, it didn't go so good. I shot- I had to kill…" He paused, and tried to calm his jangling nerves. "I killed Macalister with a gun. He was about to shoot Mazik. It wasn't good."

"Oh no," Eissa said. "Oh, sweetie, I didn't know."

"He got shot, too," Bob said. "Apparently he has a bulletproof vest on."

Eissa spun around, her brow darkening. "You got shot? Why didn't you say something? Shirt and vest off, now." She turned to one of the women who was assisting her. "Can you hold this bag of fluids for him? I need to do a quick exam."

She helped him peel the straps back and slide the vest off. It was soaked with sweat, and she tossed it aside. He was afraid to look down, but when her fingers touched his chest, he gasped.

"That's tender," he muttered, glancing at his chest. His right pectoral was swollen, with a deep red spot the size of a baseball spread across it.

"I need to see if you broke any ribs. This is going to hurt a little bit, but let me know if anything hurts really bad. Like, my hand pressure on the bruise is a two on the pain scale. Let me know if you register a seven, got it?"

Quentin gritted his teeth. "I think it's more than a two. Hurry up."

"Man up, Q. Bob got the shit kicked out of him, and you don't see him whining." She examined his torso, palpating the bruise gently despite her tough talk. After a moment, she straightened up.

"Alright, it looks like your arm got grazed, so we'll clean that up, but I don't think anything's broken. You're going to have a spectacular bruise in a day or two, though. We'll get you some ibuprofen to take the edge off, and I'll get some fluids going on you so that you're plenty hydrated."

"I'm okay," Quentin protested. "I'm drinking water, like you told me."

"You're probably in shock. I'm treating you, now sit down."

Quentin sat down. One of the women assisting her brought the supplies over, and Eissa quickly inserted a catheter in his arm. The odd sensation of the cool fluid in his vein made its way up his arm and into his chest.

"You two are going to be a great team," Bob said. "I think you've proved that here."

"You didn't see me falling apart twenty different times before we found you," Quentin said. "I was a basket case the whole time."

"Oh, I doubt that."

Quentin leaned up on his elbows and looked around at them. "I'm serious. I had to go back to the cabin to get the stuff to cauterize that guy, so he didn't bleed to death. I almost didn't come back."

It didn't seem like he could be taken very seriously while laying back, so he sat up carefully. "When I was at the DimGate, I realized I could just go home, just run away and not deal with any of this. I even set the panel for our home dimension, and activated it."

"Oh my God," Eissa said. "You were going to abandon me?"

"That's what I'm trying to tell you," Quentin said, his voice choked up. "I'm not cut out for this. I'm not a hero."

"How was it when you went into your dimension?" Bob asked.

Quentin looked down and shook his head. "I didn't open the door. I knew that guy was laying there bleeding, and Eissa needed the stuff. I chickened out at the last second."

"Hhmm," Bob grunted. "So, in a moment of incredible stress, you set aside your personal desire to run, and did what needed to be done for the good of others. What do you think, Tocho? Sounds pretty heroic to me."

"I think so, too. All the elements are there."

"You're missing the point!" Quentin cried. "I panicked, I froze, I wanted out so bad I couldn't stand it."

"Do you think that heroes don't deal with emotional conflict?" Bob asked. "That's what makes them heroes. That's what makes you a hero. Killing Macalister doesn't make you a hero. The urge to run doesn't make you a coward. It's all about overcoming those things, and still being a good guy on the other side of it."

"Bob and I have cried ourselves to sleep a thousand times," Tocho said. "We're not any tougher than you are. We've just been doing this longer, that's all. If you didn't have a heart, then you wouldn't be the guy for the job."

"You guys are frying my brain," Eissa said. "I want to go back to the part where you were going to leave me standing here."

"Nah, let it go," Tocho said. "He's beating himself up worse than you ever could. Right now, he needs you to tell him that he's okay."

"Of course, he's okay, I just want to give him some shit about it." She ruffled Quentin's hair, and pushed him back down on the ground. "Lay back, you're crimping the catheter."

"I get what you guys are saying, but I still feel shitty about people dying. I wish there was a way to get rid of that part." He stretched out on the ground and straightened his arm.

"You're going to agonize about it for a while," Tocho said. "That's part of it. You couldn't do this kind of thing if you were a sociopath, because you wouldn't care about the Bribri, either. Does that make sense?"

Quentin stared up at the deep blue sky overhead as he absorbed the idea. It seemed like a bit of a catch-22. He had to care in order to do it in the first place, but caring is what made it painful. It seemed like a significant design flaw.

"Maybe I can find a hypnotist that can block out the bad parts," he said at last. "It seems like there ought to be some way to make it bearable to right the world's wrongs, you know?"

Bob laughed, causing others around them to look over. "If you find somebody that can do that, you let me know. Then we'll use the time machine function on the DimGate, and go back and save ourselves a lifetime of pain and suffering."

"Yes," Tocho said, clapping his hands. "Now you're talking!"

Bob reached over and grasped Quentin by the wrist, and looked him in the eye. "You're going through all of this because you're a good guy, Quentin. I want to make sure you understand that. You aren't broken, and you didn't fail. You take the losses to heart because you care about people. If you didn't feel bad right now, then there would be something wrong with you."

Quentin wiped the tears away with his free hand, and tried to smile. His throat closed every time he tried to say something is response, so he just laid back and looked at the sky.

Eissa moved among them, checking the level of the fluids in their IV bags. "So, when are we going back to the island?"

"The sooner we are out of the way, the sooner they can start putting their new life together," Bob said. "We'll have to come back in a day or two and see how things are going, maybe give some advice, but we can head back any time you all are ready."

"I'll need to check the wounds on these guys a few times a day, for a few days. I also need to bring back some more drugs." Eissa disconnected the tube from Tocho's catheter. "All set. I'm out of tape though, so you'll have to hold the gauze on there once I pull the catheter."

Tocho nodded, and took the gauze from her.

"They're going to need more bandaging material, too. We have to do a medical supply run somewhere, and soon."

"We'll get your medical stuff first," Tocho said. "Then I'm going on a household goods supply run. I'm not spending my retirement sleeping on that cot at the cabin. I want a real bed."

"Yeah, me too," Bob said. "I think it's time to do a lot of upgrades to the cabin. We need more hot water, for one thing, so we need another black barrel for the roof. I'm going to take a hot shower every day for the next month."

"Wait a minute," Quentin said. "Retirement? After all this talk about dealing with feelings and being the good guys, and now we're retiring?"

"We," Bob said, pointing to Tocho and himself. "Not the papal we." He pointed at Quentin and Eissa.

"I don't get it," Quentin said. "This whole thing was a debacle without you. You can't just leave us hanging here."

"The biggest liability in this whole operation was the two of us," Bob said. "We made bad decisions, we got captured by the enemy, and we could have compromised the entire operation if you had decided to try to rescue us, instead of continuing the mission."

"And we're getting old," Tocho added. "Sitting in that shed was a hell of a lot harder on us than it would have been twenty years ago. I don't ever want to do that again."

"Besides, you proved you can handle things without us," Bob said, picking back up. "You ran this whole thing by yourselves. And with us being at the cabin, you can use us as consultants, so we'll still be involved. We just won't be slowing you down next time."

Quentin shook his head. "We need to get you back to the cabin, and maybe to a hospital or something. You're both acting delusional. I think you've probably suffered a head injury or something."

Tocho grinned. "Well, I did get kicked in the head."

"You'll have to wait until everyone's hydrated," Eissa said. "Right now, no one's going anywhere. Medic's orders."

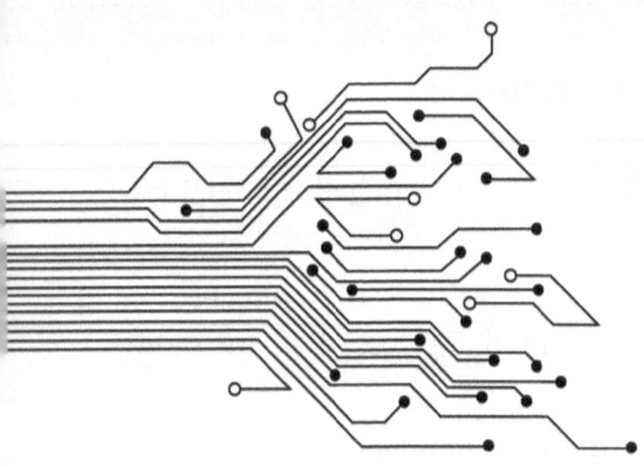

CHAPTER 21

Two weeks of sitting on the cabin porch and whittling had done wonders for Bob's face. Both of his eyes were open again, though one slightly more than the other. The bruising on his cheek had gone from blue to purple to black, then greenish and yellow around the edges as it began to shrink.

Quentin had started sitting with him in the afternoons lately, and he found their philosophical discussions to be both challenging and intellectually stimulating.

It was raining, and the cool breeze that drifted across the porch misted them from time to time. It was a welcome change after the heat of the past week.

The stick that Bob was whittling on had slowly turned into a large spoon. He was currently carving a bunch of grapes into the handle. Quentin smirked at the mess of shavings in Bob's beard.

"So, Tocho's really getting into this whole cabin upgrade thing, huh?"

Bob paused, and combed his beard out with his fingers. "We should have set this place up proper a long time ago. It's a great place to live, especially if you have a door that will take you anywhere you want to go."

"Agreed."

Bob resumed whittling. Quentin watched the rain, his thoughts swirling.

"Tell me about some of the really strange dimensions out there. What's happened in the places that are more advanced than ours?"

Bob held the spoon up to his good eye and inspected the grapes. "Oh, there're some strange ones. Let's see… as far as outright different, there's a dimension I've heard of where their brains evolved past where ours are at. Supposedly they can do things with their brain that would be considered magic pretty much anywhere else."

"You haven't been there?"

"No, that's one I heard about in a prison camp I was in for a while. I never did go there. Afraid, I guess, but I mostly was kind of skeptical about the whole thing."

"What kind of stuff could they do?"

"Oh, general telekinesis stuff, moving things around, that sort of thing."

"Huh." Quentin pushed his feet against the footstool, setting the chair to rocking again. "Do you think it's possible?"

"Well, there's a whole lot about the brain that is unknown, so I'd be hard pressed to say it's not possible, but it's a long stretch for an old logic guy like me."

"I'd like to check that out someday. What other kinds of weird things are there out there?"

"Oh, there's dimensions that are way farther along with space travel than yours, and some that are like a combination of really old and futuristic technologies. A lot of the dims from the Roman Empire timeline are like that."

"The Roman Empire timeline?"

Bob glanced at him. "Huh. I thought I told you about

that. Maybe it was Eissa." He inspected the spoon again, and went back to whittling. "There's a whole series of dims where the Roman Empire is still going. They run pretty much everything off steam."

"Oh, no." Quentin shook his head. "Steampunk is real."

Bob raised his eyebrows.

"Oh, there's a subculture in our Dim that likes to imagine what the world would be like if everything ran off steam. They have some pretty crazy ideas."

"Maybe not so crazy, huh?" Bob chuckled.

"Maybe not."

"There's a lot to learn out there," Bob said. "One of the things you'll learn is that there aren't very many absolutes. Just because something doesn't exist in your Dim doesn't mean that it doesn't exist somewhere else."

"That's a pretty open-ended concept."

"In a world of endless dimensions, there are endless possibilities," Bob said. "The more you learn, the more you realize just how little you know."

"Well, I'm ready to go explore some of it."

"Me too," Eissa said, coming around the corner. She was carrying a basket of vegetables from the garden, and Tocho was right behind her with a bucket of water. "Where are we going next?"

The End

If you enjoyed this book, please leave a review wherever you purchased it, and tell your friends about it! Quentin and Eissa need your help to take down DimCorp one element at a time, and you can help by spreading the word about the DimWorld series. Visit JBoydLong.com to sign up for notifications about upcoming book releases, and connect with the author on Facebook and Instagram @JBoydLong.

Acknowledgements

Somewhere in the neighborhood of 13.8 billion years ago, a massive explosion took place. Particles of matter were flung in every direction and have been traveling through space and time ever since. A very particular series of events occurred to bring all the right pieces together to form my incredible wife, Erica Lacher, who became the center of my universe in 2014. Without her, nothing in my world would be what it is, and I have endless gratitude for her love and support.

Kristen Sketchley was willing to play the what-if game with me regarding battlefield bullet-wound care. I hope it never happens, but if I get shot out in the jungle somewhere, I hope she's there to rescue me. Her wealth of experience and knowledge in this area is impressive, and any mistakes that appear in this book regarding medical care are mine, and not hers.

I would also like to thank Google for making fact-finding and research so much more than it was before they began doing that voodoo that they do. I based all the tech stuff in this book on real scientific research that's happening in our dimension, which I never would have known existed without the wonders of the internet. Oh, you didn't know that there was a way to manipulate matter with your brainwaves? Yes, it's happening. They're not quite to micro movers yet, but give it time.

Heather Whitaker and Kathy Rothenberger have committed a great deal of time to helping me get the story straight and all the words in the right order. I'm exceptionally grateful for their help. Perhaps if I had paid more attention in high school English class, I might be a little better at this stuff. Anyway, one of the keys to success is to surround yourself with people who are great at the stuff you are bad at, and I have a good circle of great people. I highly recommend having one.

Lastly, and perhaps most importantly, I would like to thank you for taking time out of your life to read this series of books. It means a lot to me!

About the Author

J. Boyd Long is a self-embracing nerd who loves crunching numbers, researching interesting things, and listening to podcasts, in addition to reading loads of books. His exposure to Stephen King's books at the age of 10 probably stunted him in some way, but he is still determined to leave the world a better place than he found it. He lives near Gainesville, Florida on a small farm with his incredible wife, 7 horses, 5 cats, 2 donkeys, 2 dogs, and a sheep named Gerald.

www.ingramcontent.com/pod-product-compliance
Lightning Source LLC
Chambersburg PA
CBHW050346190726
48284CB00007BB/2164